AS LONG AS WE'RE TOGETHER

AS LONG AS WE'RE TOGETHER

Adapted by Alexa Young

Based on the series created by Terri Minsky

Part One is based on the episode "I Wanna Hold Your Wristband," written by Sam Wolfson.

Part Two is based on the episode "Perfect Day 2.0," written by Erin Dunlap.

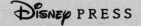 PRESS

Los Angeles • New York

Printed in the United States of America
First Paperback Edition, March 2019
1 3 5 7 9 10 8 6 4 2
Library of Congress Control Number: 2018962684
ISBN 978-1-368-02680-2
FAC-025438-19025

For more Disney Press fun, visit www.disneybooks.com
Visit DisneyChannel.com

SUSTAINABLE
FORESTRY
INITIATIVE

Certified Chain of Custody
Promoting Sustainable Forestry

www.sfiprogram.org
SFI-01054

The SFI label applies to the text stock

PART ONE

CHAPTER 1

It was an unusually sunny morning in Shadyside, but Andi Mack was feeling anything but cheery as she walked to Jefferson Middle School with her two best friends on either side of her. For the last few days, Andi had been stressing out over what she hoped was just a minor issue. But she knew she needed to talk the problem through with someone. So, trying to act casual, she glanced at Cyrus Goodman on her left, and then at Buffy Driscoll on her right. She took a deep breath and opened her mouth, determined to tell them what was on her mind.

But then, noticing a tableful of boys finishing up some homework in front of school, Andi quickly pressed her lips back together. What if those guys overheard her and laughed? What if *Buffy and Cyrus* laughed at her little—or what she hoped was a little—problem?

They're your best friends, Andi tried to reassure herself. *They would never make fun of you!*

Again, Andi glanced at Cyrus. Not only was he reliable beyond belief, but he was the kind of friend who was always ready to offer a wise word—or, at least, what *he* thought was a wise word. The best thing about Cyrus, though, was that he had this quirky way of looking at life that never ceased to make his friends laugh. Then Andi looked at Buffy—the one in their group who always spoke her mind, constantly pushing everyone around her to be a bit bolder, a bit tougher. Plus, she always had Andi's back. She would totally serve up the pep talk Andi needed.

Yes. Andi nodded to herself. Between the two of them, Cyrus and Buffy would definitely be able to help. So without giving it another thought, she went ahead and blurted out that she had to ask them a question.

"Lay it on us," Buffy quickly replied, an invincible

look in her big brown eyes, and Andi knew she'd come to the right place. Buffy loved solving problems. She was a total overachiever—in school, in sports, in *life*. She would probably have more answers than Andi even had questions . . . especially considering Andi really only had one.

So Andi clenched her fists, took a deep breath, and tried not to sound too desperate as the words finally tumbled out of her mouth. "Should Jonah and I be holding hands by now?"

Buffy was about to respond, but before she could, Cyrus's arm shot out and he placed a hand on Andi's shoulder, stepping in front of the girls to stop them in their tracks. "I'd better take this one," he said, arching one dark eyebrow and smiling without a hint of irony, let alone humility. "I mean, I *am* the only one with . . . *hands-on* hand-holding experience."

Buffy rolled her eyes, but she and Andi both had to admit that Cyrus was technically right—he had been on at least a couple of real dates with Iris. It felt weird even to think about Cyrus in a romantic relationship, not to mention with someone who was two years older.

Iris was an actual *high school freshman*, and she also happened to be best friends with Jonah's ex-girlfriend, Amber, which was how Cyrus had met her. Yeah, it was complicated—but not nearly as complicated as Andi's current dilemma.

Seriously. Why hadn't Jonah even *attempted* to hold her hand in the weeks since he'd broken up with Amber? He certainly acted like he wanted to be with Andi, and he'd had plenty of opportunities to make a hand-holding move. It was something Andi had pictured in her mind a million times. After all, *the* Jonah Beck was her longtime crush—an eighth grader whom she never would have expected to become her friend, let alone something more serious than that. But then Bex had set up a surprise Frisbee lesson with Jonah for Andi's thirteenth birthday. And as truly shocking (not to mention mortifying) as that lesson had been, the bigger surprise had been the undeniable spark between Andi and Jonah.

After that, Jonah asked Andi to join the Ultimate Frisbee team, and he and Andi started spending more time together. And the more time they spent together, the more they realized they liked each other. A lot. So although there had been plenty of bumps along the way—including all the stuff with Amber—Andi and Jonah seemed to be moving toward coupledom. But if they *were* a real couple, Andi had to wonder why he wasn't he holding her hand. Was he scared? Embarrassed? Or was there . . . *something wrong with Andi?*

This was precisely why she needed to discuss it with Buffy and Cyrus. Every time she started to think about Jonah's hand holding her hand—or, well, *not* holding her hand—she felt like her head was going to explode. She shot a pleading look at Cyrus, beyond ready for him to bestow his wealth of hand-holding wisdom upon her.

"May I see your hand, please?" Cyrus asked, and Andi reluctantly held it out for Cyrus to inspect, which he proceeded to do with all the focus and care of a skilled—if slightly mad—scientist. "Hmmm . . . healthy nail beds, no calluses, good-sized knuckles!" Impressed with his findings, Cyrus grinned and locked eyes with Andi, then offered his formal diagnosis: "I don't see any reason not to be holding this hand."

Relieved as Andi was, she still frowned. "And yet, he isn't holding it."

Cyrus nodded sympathetically but then held up an index finger. "Perhaps you suffer from hyperhidrosis."

Andi wrinkled her nose and turned to look at Buffy, who appeared to be just as confused as Andi.

Cyrus widened his eyes, amazed that his friends had no idea what he was talking about. "Sweaty palms?" he clarified.

Andi inspected her hands. "They don't look sweaty." She rubbed her palms together. "They don't *feel* sweaty."

Cyrus gently grabbed Andi by the wrists and tried to explain, with as much patience as he could muster. "You're not nervous when you hold your *own* hand."

"So, if I'm holding Jonah's hand . . ." Andi suddenly gasped, her heart beginning to race as it dawned on her. "It can just *happen*?"

"Hyperhidrosis is a cruel mistress," Cyrus said with a sigh, adjusting the strap on his beige cross-body messenger bag.

But Buffy was done listening to Cyrus, and she

decided Andi should be, too. "If you want to hold Jonah's hand, *hold Jonah's hand*," she counseled forcefully, putting an arm around Andi and guiding her toward the front of the school. "Don't wait for *him* to instigate, just go for it!"

At that very moment, as fate would have it, Andi looked up and discovered Jonah walking directly toward her.

"Here he comes now," Buffy whispered, a sly smile crossing her lips.

Andi sucked in her breath and realized her hands were already starting to perspire a bit—and how could they not, given how hot it was? And by *hot*, Andi mostly meant Jonah. He looked so cute in his gray-and-green-striped hoodie, his backpack draped casually over one shoulder, his brown hair flopping into his spectacularly blue eyes. But the best part was that when Jonah noticed Andi, his whole face lit up. His eyes seemed extra sparkly that morning, and the dimples in his cheeks looked especially . . . dimply.

As Andi and Jonah walked toward each other, practically in slow motion, Andi rubbed a palm on her black-and-white-checkered pants, and once she was certain she'd conquered any possible hint of hyperhidrosis, she wiggled her fingers in anticipation, like a gunfighter before a duel. Finally, when she and Jonah were almost close enough to touch, Andi reached out her hand—and Jonah did, too.

Andi grinned. It was going to happen. They were going to hold hands at last!

"Andi." A clipboard suddenly shot between Andi and Jonah, preventing them from making contact. Andi's heart sank as she looked up to see Dr. Metcalf, the silver-haired school principal, looking especially strict that morning in a gray suit with a purple tie. "We're trying something different today. Please step over to the table marked *A*."

Andi spun around to see two office workers sitting behind tables in front of the school's main building. One table was draped in a blue tablecloth and had a sign emblazoned with a large black *A*, and the other had an orange tablecloth with a *B* sign on it.

"Jonah, you're over there at the *B* table," Dr. Metcalf added with a casual wave of his hand.

Andi and Jonah furrowed their brows in confusion, but then Andi had an idea. She turned to the principal. "Can I be at the *B* table, too?"

Dr. Metcalf leaned down, stared into Andi's eyes like she was all of two years old, and said, "No, you cannot." Then he tersely motioned for her to hurry along before turning to direct the rest of her class-mates. "Buffy, you go to *B*. Cyrus, you're at the *A* table. Everybody, come on. Denise, *B*. Erin, *A*. Farrah, *B* . . ."

Andi and her friends were all given plastic wristbands—Andi and Cyrus sported neon-green ones marked with *A*, and Jonah's and Buffy's were orange and marked with *B*s—and they searched each other's faces for some sort of explanation.

"Wristbands. Are we going somewhere?" Cyrus wondered, genuinely concerned that perhaps there was a field trip he'd forgotten about. He hadn't brought a brown-bag lunch that day, which could mean serious trouble, given his history of hypoglycemia.

Jonah shrugged and turned to look at Andi, his lips curving into a pout. "Why can't we be in the same group?"

Andi shook her head and sighed. "Maybe someone in your group will switch?" She rose up onto her toes and searched the crowd of students for potential candidates.

But once again, Dr. Metcalf shut her down, his voice laced with condescension. "Andi, these groups are not random. They were chosen according to very specific guidelines."

Buffy stepped in and tossed her long curly hair, then narrowed her eyes at the principal like she was challenging him to a duel. "Which are?"

"Um, let me see. . . ." Dr. Metcalf looked down and riffled through the papers on his clipboard, laughing briefly as he found what he was looking for, but then matching Buffy's hostile stare and snapping, "None of your business!"

Buffy hooked her thumbs into the front pockets of her wide-legged jeans and shot daggers at the principal, who simply turned his attention to the rest of the students. "Everybody, stay with your group!" he called out to them. "No intermingling. It's very important!"

Then, before Buffy and Andi could even attempt to

speak to each other, Dr. Metcalf glared at them again and waved his clipboard threateningly. *"Stay with your group!"*

So though they had absolutely no idea why, Andi and Cyrus headed toward the glass doors to the school that were marked with another *A* sign, while Buffy and Jonah made their way to the ones marked *B*.

They all felt defeated. It was obvious the principal was on some sort of twisted, controlling mission—and, at least for the moment, there was nothing they could do except fall into line . . . or, well, two *separate* lines.

CHAPTER 2

When they got to their first class of the day, Andi, Buffy, and Cyrus discovered that all the desks had been separated into two groups, too—and everyone with a green *A* wristband was directed to one side of the room, while those with orange *B* wristbands were expected to sit on the opposite side.

"Pop quiz," Mr. Plimpton said wearily, setting down a paper in front of each student in the *A* group and then dumping a large stack of thick booklets on Buffy's desk. "When you finish, you're free to go."

Andi looked down at the single sheet of paper, started working on it for a moment, then spun around to look at Cyrus. "*This* is our pop quiz?" she scoffed. She couldn't help it. "A connect-the-dots puzzle?"

"Apparently." Cyrus shrugged and dutifully returned his attention to the paper. A pop quiz was a pop quiz, and who was he to question authority— especially when said authority was making his life *easier* for a change?

But Buffy, who was on the other side of the aisle, frowned at Andi and craned her neck to get a better look at Group A's pop quiz. "Wait . . . *I* didn't get a connect-the-dots puzzle."

"What'd you get?" Andi asked, even more confused now.

"A twenty-page booklet of math proofs." Buffy held up the packet and flipped through it, her cheeks angrily flushing as pink as her sleeveless top. "And this is *English!*"

Andi smacked her hands down on her desk and widened her eyes at Mr. Plimpton, who was now sitting on the edge of his own desk at the front of the class-room. "Why'd we get different tests?" she demanded.

The teacher slowly closed his eyes, shook his head, and sighed. "I am seven years from retirement," he muttered, barely reopening his eyes to stare down into his mug of coffee as he blew into it. "Just do the work."

Andi exhaled loudly, beyond frustrated, but turned her attention back to her puzzle. Meanwhile, Buffy—never one to back down from a challenge, even one as obviously irrational as this—tossed a haughty look at her friends and quipped, "I guess we're the smarter group."

Cyrus glared at Buffy but continued to work on his puzzle until, a few desks over, a redheaded classmate named Gus held up his paper, his eyes blinking behind his dark-rimmed glasses. "It's a baby giraffe!" he said so enthusiastically that saliva sprayed through his braces. "Look!"

Buffy rolled her eyes and sneered, "Group A's finest." Then, annoyed as she was, she dove into the packet of math problems with even more fortitude.

Moments later, Andi and the rest of Group A completed their puzzles, handed them in, and began filing out of the classroom—except for Cyrus, who couldn't resist stopping at Buffy's desk, eager to rectify her earlier comment regarding the intellectual superiority of Group B. "Buffy, *your* GPA isn't that much higher than Andi's and mine," he pointed out, raising his dark eyebrows at her.

Undeterred, Buffy glared at the connect-the-dots puzzle Cyrus still had in his hands and scoffed. "Your baby giraffe has five legs."

Cyrus did a quick double take at his paper and scowled when he realized his friend was right. Not that it mattered. Mr. Plimpton had said that when they were finished with their quizzes, they were free to go—which meant that while Buffy would be stuck working on torturous math proofs for the rest of the period, Cyrus and Andi were already out of there.

CHAPTER 3

While Andi was in her morning classes, Rebecca Mack—a.k.a. Bex—pulled into her parents' driveway on her motorcycle. It was a scene reminiscent of that day not long before when she had returned to Shadyside, just before Andi's thirteenth birthday, to finally reveal the truth: that she wasn't Andi's older sister, as Andi had always believed, but in fact her *mother*. That meant that Celia and Ham, who had raised Andi all those years, were actually her *grandparents*. As shocking as the news had been, everyone involved had been doing their best to adjust to the situation—including Bowie Quinn, Bex's free-spirited high school boyfriend . . . who was Andi's father.

18

In fact, Bowie had adjusted so well that he'd practically become a regular fixture at the Mack house. With his incredible cooking skills, not to mention his miraculous ability to nurture practically any plant, he had even achieved what Bex had once believed to be her own personal mission impossible: he had totally and completely won over Celia, Andi's grandmother—whom she was *not* to call Grandma, but CeCe. So it wasn't all that surprising that when Bex pulled up in front of the house that day, she found Bowie working on CeCe's beloved flower bed in the front garden.

"Wow!" Bex said as she climbed off her motorcycle and unstrapped her helmet. She pulled it off and headed over to take a closer look at Bowie's landscaping skills. As always, Bex was the picture of cool. Her dark wavy hair was pulled up into a messy bun, and she wore one of her standard outfits: a turquoise choker and a long silver chain around her neck, distressed jeans, heavy boots, and a classic concert tee beneath her black leather motorcycle jacket.

Bowie shook his chin-length curls and flashed a goofy grin before returning his attention to the flower bed. Until Bex had returned to town, he'd been living his dream as a touring musician, playing guitar with the Renaissance Boys. But the moment he discovered he was a father and got the chance to meet Andi, he decided to stick around so he could spend more time with her . . . and with Bex. Bowie had even proposed to Bex, but much to his dismay—and Andi's—Bex turned him down. Still, they were all finding a way to be their own version of a family. Bowie had even decided to put down roots, literally, by getting a job at the local nursery, Judy's Blooms, which thrilled CeCe to no end. To her, it was the next best thing to being a doctor.

"You like it?" Bowie asked Bex, sounding nervous as he studied the wood chips, which he had meticulously placed around a large group of bushes. "I wasn't sure if I should go with the pine bark or the spruce bark."

Bex couldn't help laughing at how seriously Bowie was taking this particular gardening gig. But she also understood why he was worried. Even though the bark and plants looked as flawless as every other inch of the front garden, and even though CeCe now loved Bowie more than any other guy Bex had ever brought home—and, well, maybe even more than she loved Bex herself—she was still CeCe . . . and trying to meet the woman's painfully high expectations could be downright scary.

Still, Bex offered Bowie her most reassuring smile. "Well, I have no idea which bark I'm looking at, but . . . excellent choice."

"Spruce bark!" CeCe clucked approvingly as she emerged from the house and walked across the lush green lawn. Like the impeccably manicured yard, and even while dressed for yard work, Bex's mother looked perfect as ever in her dark slacks and a royal blue button-down top.

Bowie smiled, relieved that CeCe sounded impressed. He stood up and pulled off his yellow gardening gloves, then shoved them into the back pocket of his jeans. "It felt right."

Bex had to agree. It did feel right, and as she looked around and realized how much work CeCe was having

Bowie put into this landscaping job, her heart filled with hope. "So! This is a good sign!" Bex said, flashing a wide smile.

"What is?" CeCe asked, narrowing her eyes at her daughter.

"You're fixing up the yard," Bex explained, waving her arms around excitedly. "That means you're not selling the house!"

Ever since CeCe had dropped that bombshell, Bex had been walking around with what felt like the weight of the world on her shoulders. It wasn't that Bex was bummed about her parents' deciding to sell their place, per se, but it had been the only home Andi had ever known for the first thirteen years of her life. Even now that Andi and Bex had an apartment of their own, few things made Andi quite as happy as returning to the Mack house—or, more specifically, to Andi Shack. That miniature house with the quaint front porch was where Andi went when she wanted to create her incredible crafts or simply be alone with her thoughts.

Bex couldn't imagine anything worse than telling Andi that the house—including Andi Shack—would be sold. But in fact, CeCe *had* saddled Bex with the task of breaking the news to Andi . . . which Bex hadn't quite gotten around to doing yet. And boy, was she glad she hadn't, because now it looked like she wouldn't have to!

CeCe peered at Bex from beneath her black visor, her eyes silently seeming to mock her. "That's *why* we're fixing up the yard. The open house is Thursday."

Bex's heart sank. She couldn't believe it. "The *what*?"

"Why do you sound so shocked?" CeCe demanded. "I *told* you I was selling the house."

"I know what you *told* me," Bex replied as she began to wring her hands. "But I never thought you'd actually *do* it!"

"Right . . . because if there's one quality I'm typically associated with, it's a lack of follow-through," CeCe scoffed, but when Bowie snickered in solidarity, he was swiftly silenced by her stern glare.

"How can you be so casual about selling our house?" Bex frowned.

"*Our* house?" CeCe began tugging on her gardening

gloves. "You moved out of this house, remember? *Twice!* What do you care if we sell it?"

"Because when Andi finds out—" Bex blurted, only to watch CeCe's face freeze furiously in disbelief. *Oh, no.* Bex's eyes darted around, as if she was searching for a hole in the ground to swallow her up. She shot a look at Bowie, silently hoping that he could quickly dig one for her.

"Wait," CeCe said, her jaw dropping open. "Why haven't you told her?"

"Because I'm in denial that it's happening," Bex replied with a pout, and then—even though her attempts at verbal manipulation had *never* worked on CeCe in the past—she decided to give it a last-ditch effort: "It's a dangerous game of chicken we're playing. If you continue, you might actually end up selling the house."

CeCe smirked, shaking her head and staring down at the ground, and for a fleeting moment Bex thought that perhaps her strategy had worked: maybe her mother *was* bluffing, and now that Bex had called her on it, she was going to show her hand. Yes! CeCe was going to admit that she was making idle threats. She didn't really want to sell the house—she just wanted to make Bex feel guilty about something. But guilty about what? Taking her own daughter away so she could finally be a responsible parent and raise her? Could that be it?

But before CeCe could confirm that any of Bex's unspoken theories were right, Bowie turned to Bex and said gently, "You really need to tell Andi."

"Are you kidding?" Bex fired back. Sometimes she really wished Bowie and CeCe *hadn't* hit it off so well. "She's gonna be crushed."

"She's tougher than you know. She'll be fine," CeCe interjected flatly, as if she knew Bex's own daughter better than Bex did—which, to be fair, might have been true in some cases. But not in this one. *Definitely* not in this one.

"She's losing Andi Shack!" Bex couldn't help raising her voice. She didn't care if she was being melodramatic. She felt like she was channeling her former adolescent self *and* Andi at the same time. "She's *not* going to be fine!"

But true to form, CeCe failed to realize the gravity of the situation. "Andi Shack is wherever Andi is," she insisted, as if she'd never been a teenager herself—and, truth be told, Bex often wondered if CeCe had skipped right past that stage. "Take the sign and make a new one."

"It's not going to be that easy, and you know it!" Now Bex was yelling. She couldn't help it. How could her mother just stand there with her hands on her hips and act so oblivious? Sure, CeCe had been that way when it came to what would make Bex happy, but this was different . . . and this wasn't only about Andi's happiness; it was about Andi's entire *life*!

Then, adding insult to injury, Bowie held up his hands at Bex and CeCe and said, "Can we all just take a breath?"

What? Bex spun around to glare at Bowie, yelling at him now, too. "And you! I can't believe you're helping her!"

Bowie's mouth fell open and he looked at Bex with wounded eyes. For a fleeting moment, she thought maybe she was being too hard on him. But even after glancing around at all the effort he'd put into the yard and acknowledging that his work was exquisite, she couldn't help pointing out that he was on the side of evil.

"Evil!" Bex shouted, pointing an accusatory finger at Bowie as she charged to her motorcycle. She tugged on her helmet and revved the engine so it growled at her mother and Bowie like a dutiful ally—the only one she apparently had at the moment—and then sped off.

CeCe sighed. She shook her head and actually looked like she felt the slightest bit guilty, which made Bowie feel sort of guilty himself. Still reeling from Bex's yelling at him, he suddenly didn't know where to turn, so he simply fixed his gaze on the bark he'd agonized over for hours.

But once Bex's bike had disappeared down the road, CeCe's face brightened, and she smiled at Bowie. "I'm on the side of the market that's up five percent!" she pointed out giddily.

Of course, Bowie knew it wasn't all about the money for CeCe; he knew that she and Ham simply didn't need so much space now that Andi had moved out of the house and in with Bex. At the same time, though, he knew Bex was right: Andi was probably going to be seriously bummed about losing Andi Shack. But she would get over it, like CeCe said . . . wouldn't she? The more Bowie thought about what Bex had said about Andi being crushed, the more he could almost feel his daughter's devastation. Deep down, he knew that all Bex was trying to do was protect Andi, keep her safe and happy—and as Andi's father, didn't he have that job, too?

Bowie frowned. He glanced at CeCe again and felt another pang of guilt. Was Bex right to be so mad at him? *Was* he on the side of evil? Now that he'd put it all together, Bowie felt like a line had been drawn in the sand—or at least in the spruce bark—and he was going to have to choose a side.

As if choosing between pine and spruce hadn't already been hard enough!

CHAPTER 4

Back at school, Cyrus and Buffy were in PE class—and as in all the other classes that day, they were separated. The Group A kids, including Cyrus, were on one side of the gym, while Group B, with Buffy, was on the other.

The gym teacher, decked out in his blue gym shorts and red T-shirt, wheeled a rack with a dozen red playground balls across the shiny wood floor. Then he blew his whistle and marched between the two groups of kids, eyes widening with maniacal enthusiasm behind his glasses as he growled, "Okay! Who wants to play some *DODGEBALL*?" He sounded like a sports announcer riling up the crowd before a major heavyweight boxing match.

But while most of the kids seemed elated, clapping, cheering, and pumping their fists in the air, Cyrus turned fifty shades of pale. "Cheers the bloodthirsty mob," he mumbled under his breath as he nervously glanced around at his classmates.

That was when the coach raised his arm and, with a flourish, presented a long strip of black material. "Group B," he said with a grin, "you'll be wearing these."

"*Blindfolds?*" Buffy balked and spun around to see if the other kids in her group were equally outraged.

Cyrus, on the other hand, was stoked! No longer thinking about the pain all those balls would inflict when mercilessly hurled at him, he slowly nodded and whispered, "Ooh, a twist!" before turning to high-five one of the girls on his team.

As Buffy and the other kids in Group B tried to voice their dissent, the coach just shook his head and shoved the blindfolds at them. "Come on." He snickered, handing the dark scarves out one by one while mocking their disappointed pouts. "There's no crying in dodgeball!"

• • •

In the school hallway, Andi was sitting in a sectioned-off lounge area that was partly concealed by a giant sign indicating it was off-limits to Group B. She sighed happily as a woman in a black spa uniform finished up the best shoulder massage Andi had ever had. Andi then wandered out into the hallway to see what other perks were on offer—and, more specifically, to find the waiter who had taken her order for a smoothie several minutes earlier. That was when she noticed a bunch of Group B kids, including Jonah, trying to maneuver long-handled paint rollers over the hallway walls.

She also noticed Dr. Metcalf farther down the hall, making sure nobody from Group B was wandering into one of the exclusive Group A zones. But when the principal finally disappeared from view, Andi ran over and loud-whispered Jonah's name, then waved her hand at the wall and asked him what was going on.

"Art class," he explained with a shrug, carefully moving his roller up and down and laughing in spite of himself. "Although I'm not sure how painting a wall the same color teaches us anything about art."

Andi cringed. The whole day had been so weird, but she had resigned herself to the fact that they weren't going to get any logical explanations from the principal or their teachers—at least, not yet.

"What are you doing here?" Jonah glanced over at Andi while dipping his paint roller into a metal tin on the floor.

"Oh, uh . . ." Andi wasn't sure if she should tell Jonah, but how else could she explain it away? "I've got a forty-five-minute hall pass, so I'm just killing time before my foot massage."

Jonah's blue eyes practically doubled in size and seemed to turn green . . . with envy. "Group A gets *foot massages*?"

Before Andi could respond, the waiter who'd taken her smoothie order reappeared with a trayful of cups. He wore black pants and a black tie with a crisp white button-down shirt. "Your smoothie," he said, handing a cup to Andi.

"Thank you." Andi grinned and took a sip, then

noticed Jonah looking at her like an injured puppy. She frowned and stared down at the cup. "This is wrong."

"I know," Jonah said with a scowl, narrowing his eyes at Andi. His voice betrayed a mixture of hurt, confusion, and irritation. "Why's your group getting special treatment?"

"I . . . meant the smoothie," Andi said sheepishly, turning around to get the attention of the waiter, who dutifully returned to her side. "I ordered the strawberry-banana."

After the waiter swapped out her cup for a different one, Andi took a sip and then looked back at Jonah, who was now glaring at her like she had committed an unforgivable crime.

"But this, too . . . also wrong," Andi finally acknowledged, gesturing at the wall Jonah was still painting, even as he continued to stare at her with those big sad eyes. Then, noticing Dr. Metcalf peering at her down the hall, Andi remembered she wasn't supposed to be interacting with anyone from Group B. So even though she wished she could figure out a way to help

Jonah—to make all the inequity of the day disappear—she instead carefully backed away while frowning apologetically. She felt terrible, but what could she do?

Maybe she would come up with a plan during her foot massage.

• • •

Meanwhile, the dodgeball game in the gym was underway, and Cyrus was killing it! He chucked a ball at one of the blindfolded Group B players and it slammed into her shoulder, knocking her out of the game. Then he grabbed another ball and sent it flying hard and fast into the legs of a Group B kid, forcing him to buckle and fall to the ground.

"Yes!" Cyrus grunted like a bona fide jock, his eyes flashing with newfound competitive grit as the Group B players frantically tried to avoid his skillful throws. "Buffy, I wish you could see this! I have great hand-eye coordination!"

Buffy was still in the game, somehow managing to dodge every last ball, even while visually restricted. "So do I, and I'm *blindfolded*!" she shouted at Cyrus, miraculously catching a ball as it flew directly at her.

"Actually, Buffy, *I'm* the one who's been blindfolded—*metaphorically*," Cyrus pointed out, unable to conceal his burgeoning love of the game as the gym teacher walked over to him with a fiery look in his eyes, shoved a ball into Cyrus's hands, and gave him an encouraging pat on the back. "My whole life I didn't think I could play sports!"

Little did Cyrus know—although he probably could have assumed—that behind her blindfold, Buffy was rolling her eyes. "You were right," she fired back at him.

"Silence, B!" Cyrus commanded with a snarl. Then, with even more athletic prowess, he raised his arms overhead and hurled the ball, nailing Buffy right in her upper back.

Yes! That was it! Cyrus had proven himself to be the better athlete—something neither he nor Buffy had ever imagined they would see in this lifetime.

And as much as she didn't *want* to see it, Buffy pulled off her blindfold and furiously shot a look of disgust at Cyrus. Unfazed, he simply grinned and motioned for her to get off the court. She was out, he was still in, and everything was right with the world. Or at least, everything was right with Group A's world.

CHAPTER 5

Later that day, back at the apartment, Bex was desperate for some comfort food. It was the one thing she could count on to make her feel better after an argument with her mother—or, really, when she was upset about anything. Because this argument involved Bowie, and because it was now clearer than ever that Bex was going to have to break some seriously bad news to Andi all by herself, there was really only one comfort food that would ease Bex's suffering. But before she could pick up the phone to place her pizza order, there was a knock on the door.

Hmmm, she marveled. *Have I developed some sort of pizza-ordering psychic powers?*

Unfortunately, when Bex opened the door, instead of a pizza delivery, she found Bowie standing there, still covered in dirt and grass stains from the garden of evil.

"Oh . . ." Bex smiled with gritted teeth. "I think you have the wrong apartment. I didn't order any *betrayal*."

Bowie produced a pan from behind his back. "I brought fudge," he said, his tone apologetic.

Bex grimaced, annoyed that Bowie would attempt to manipulate her with something as obvious as chocolate. But then, as the sweet aroma reached her nose, she was rendered powerless. She couldn't possibly resist fudge, especially when it was made by a skilled cook like Bowie. It was quite possibly the only comfort food that could compete with pizza for Bex's affections.

"Fine," she said with a sigh, grabbing the pan without a hint of reluctance. "Come in."

Following Bex across the hardwood floors with the boho-chic rugs, Bowie glanced around and couldn't help noticing that Andi had already kind of turned a solid chunk of the apartment into its own version of Andi Shack. She had used long, colorful scarves to create curtains for the windows; each of the throw pillows on the olive-green velvet couch and chairs in the living room had been decorated with one of her custom designs; there were tiny paper lanterns strung up on the ceiling just like the ones in Andi Shack; and even the old yellow refrigerator had been adorned with zigzagging pieces of orange, pink, turquoise, and red duct tape. It was one of Andi's favorite supplies for embellishing practically anything.

It all added up to one thing, in Bowie's mind: even if CeCe and Ham did wind up selling the house and she no longer had the original Andi Shack, his kid was going to be okay. And it wasn't only because she would still have a home where she could do her craft projects, but because Bowie and Bex would always be there to protect her heart, to make sure she felt happy and safe and loved. That was really why Bowie had decided to head over to Bex's place—not to placate her with a chocolaty peace offering, nor to take her side, exactly . . . but to be *by* her side when she broke the news to Andi. It was only fair that Bowie shoulder some of the responsibility and help present a unified parental support team.

But before Bowie could tell Bex any of that, she spun around and—without even mentioning CeCe by name—blurted, "She doesn't even care that she's going to break Andi's heart!"

Bowie shook his head and sighed. "Of *course* she cares. A lot! That's why she wants *you* to tell her."

Bex set the fudge down on the kitchen table and questioningly arched one eyebrow.

"She can't bear to do it herself," he added.

It was true. Bowie had gotten to know CeCe pretty well over the past few months, and although he realized she and Bex had a complicated relationship that didn't always bring out CeCe's softer side, Bowie had witnessed a sensitive heart beating beneath the tough exterior. He also knew CeCe was fiercely protective of *Andi's* sensitive heart, which pretty much put them all on the same side as far as Bowie was concerned.

"Well, if it's so hard, why sell the house at all?" Bex scowled while pulling the plastic wrap off the pan, unleashing even more of the delicious aroma and sending her taste buds into a salivating tailspin.

"Because they don't need all that space," Bowie said, stating the obvious. "It's just the two of them. If they sell the house, they can live their own lives. They can travel, they can have adventures . . ."

As he trailed off, Bowie grabbed a couple of forks and set them on the table next to the fudge. Again, he realized just how much they all had in common, and determined to get that point across to Bex, he stared into her eyes and added, "Like we did."

Bex groaned and shook her head as she balled up the plastic wrap and tossed it in the sink. She hated for Bowie to be right about this. But he probably was. She shouldn't expect her parents to live in that big house all by themselves. They'd already sacrificed so much for Bex *and* for Andi, and selling the house was a call they should be allowed to make without anyone staging a rebellion. Still, she couldn't stop thinking about the fallout once Andi Shack was no longer accessible.

"I know I didn't live there for a long time, but I still

thought of it as home," Bex said, pulling a paper towel from the roll and tearing it into two pieces—one for her and one for Bowie. "And it's Andi's home. And if I'd never moved her out, they wouldn't have to sell it."

Bex shuddered as she considered what she'd just admitted. If she was being totally honest with herself, she was blaming her parents—especially CeCe—for selling the house because she didn't want to face the more difficult truth: that Bex, in fact, would be the one responsible. Worse still, there was a very real chance that when Bex finally broke the news to her, Andi would fault Bex, too. And who could blame her?

"Huh. Ironic, isn't it?" Bowie nodded as he sat across from Bex at the kitchen table. Then, about to dig into the fudge, he stopped and narrowed his eyes. "If I'm using that word right. I'm never sure."

"You are," Bex replied, scooping a piece of fudge out of the pan and taking a bite. "I think." She savored the confection, allowing it and Bowie's question to distract her, ever so briefly, from the more difficult questions on her mind. *Was* he using the word correctly? Suddenly, she wasn't sure, and Bex was usually an authority on those kinds of things. "But if you *aren't* using it correctly and I just said you were, *that* would be ironic."

Bex grinned and waved her fork at Bowie before digging back into the fudge.

"Ah!" Bowie smiled back and ate some more fudge. "Uh-huh."

"I *think*," Bex added, wrinkling her nose. "I don't know!"

They both laughed, and Bex breathed a sigh of relief. It really was nice to be discussing something as mundane as word choice with Bowie, even though she knew she couldn't avoid the inevitable for much longer. Soon enough, Bex was going to have to make some bigger word choices—namely, finding the right ones to use when she finally told Andi about CeCe and Ham selling the house.

CHAPTER 6

If things had been weird at school for the first half of the day, they got even weirder when it was time for lunch. Walking into the cafeteria, Andi and her friends discovered that that room, too, was split into two sections—this time with big yellow expandable gates running across the middle. On the side marked with Group A signs, beautiful round tables were decked out with white tablecloths, fine china, and flower arrangements, making Cyrus wonder if all the events of the day had been leading up to some sort of twisted, mysterious Bar or Bat Mitzvah bash. On the Group B side, however, were the usual wooden cafeteria tables.

A bunch of students were already enjoying their meals—or, at least, the Group A kids were, digging into a lavish spread that included giant bowls of shrimp cocktail, bread baskets full of croissants and rolls, and platters laden with fruits and vegetables, not to mention freshly carved prime rib and a deli tray of meats and cheeses. The Group B kids, on the other hand, were attempting to choke down some sort of mystery meat slop.

After Andi and Cyrus took their seats at one of the fancy tables, Cyrus immediately grabbed some shrimp, savoring each magnificent morsel as he dipped them into the tastiest cocktail sauce he'd ever had.

How can something this delicious not be kosher? he wondered to himself, chomping down on another delectable crustacean.

But Andi couldn't bring herself to eat a bite, especially when she glanced around at the stark contrast between the Group A side and the Group B side. She noticed Buffy and Jonah, looking hungry and miserable, through the diamond-shaped gaps in the gate.

That was when all the pieces of the puzzle finally

fit together in Andi's brain. "I think I know what's going on," she told Cyrus.

"What?" her friend replied, stuffing some more shrimp into his mouth.

"I bet this is some social justice thing that Metcalf dreamed up." Again, Andi looked around at the kids in Group A, who had been getting the royal treatment all day, while their Group B peers were forced to do hard labor with zero perks. "We're supposed to learn how unfair it is that some people get things and some people don't!"

"Cool," Cyrus replied without the slightest hint of empathy or understanding. He simply held up an empty silver dish and asked, "Can you pass the cock-tail sauce?"

"Cyrus, we should *do* something," Andi insisted, ignoring his condiment request.

"Like what?" Cyrus wondered, reaching across the table to take Andi's cocktail sauce.

"Like we all stand together," Andi replied, getting up and walking over to pull Cyrus out of his chair.

"And we go over to the *B* side, and we share our stuff with them!"

Now the injustices of the day were really starting to hit Andi hard, and she couldn't possibly let it continue any longer. If she didn't take a stand, who would? So, marching toward the gate dividing the two sides of the cafeteria, she readied herself to rally the troops and shouted out to Group A, "Who's with me?"

Andi smiled with all the enthusiasm she could muster, but the kids in her group either kept eating their fancy meals or stared blankly up at her.

She cringed and hung her head. "*Nobody's* with me."

● ● ●

Frustrated as Andi was, it was nothing compared to what her friends in Group B were going through. Sitting across from each other, Buffy and Jonah stared down at their inedible lunch. Jonah held up a plastic spoon, and some grayish-green slime slid off it and back down into his paper bowl. "What *is* this? It's docious-atrocious."

"Could be soup . . . could be stew," Buffy muttered,

examining the lumpy stuff on her own spoon and bringing it a bit closer to her nose, which made her stomach lurch. "Ugh! It smells like socks." Buffy pushed aside her bowl, and then, noticing Andi, who stood at the gate, gesturing frantically at Jonah, she added, "Hey, I think Andi wants to talk to you."

Jonah spun around to discover Andi, her fingers curled around the bars of the yellow gate, staring longingly at him. He immediately got up and walked toward her. He gripped the bars of the gate, too, and they stared at each other.

"I'm coming over to your side," Andi told him urgently.

"No!" Jonah protested, glancing around the cafeteria, his face clouding over with genuine fear. "It's too dangerous—there are teachers everywhere."

"I don't care!" Andi insisted.

Jonah widened his eyes and shook his head, yet he couldn't help marveling at Andi's bravery. "How will you get past the barrier?"

Looking down at the gate, which was on wheels,

Andi easily pushed it open, stepped over to Jonah's side, and closed it again.

"Um, what are you doing?" Buffy blinked incredulously at Andi after she and Jonah sat down.

"I'm not accepting the rules of this community—I'm with you guys now," Andi told her friend, crossing her arms. Then an uncomfortable chill ran down her spine. It was weird to be the daring one in that moment, when that was usually Buffy's thing. What had happened to Andi's friend? Why wasn't *she* standing up and fighting for what was right, too?

But maybe it was Andi's turn to inspire Buffy, who smiled as they turned to stare across the barrier, where Cyrus was all alone at his table, looking like he might have eaten one too many shrimp.

"Did you bring any food?" Jonah asked Andi, his voice full of quiet desperation.

"No," Andi replied, noticing that kids at the tables all around them were also hoping she'd brought something edible for them. "I left so quickly I had to leave everything behind."

As a collective groan rose from the Group B students, including Buffy and Jonah, Andi couldn't help pointing out that they were all being kind of judgy.

But that was when Cyrus picked up a huge bowlful of shrimp and headed for the yellow divider. Buffy practically clapped her hands when she saw him gesturing for someone to let him through. "Cyrus is at the gate!" she told Jonah excitedly, her face lighting up at the sight of him . . . and, more than that, at the delicious food in his hands.

Jonah slid the gate open to let Cyrus in, and the moment he arrived, Buffy began leading a chant: "Cy-rus! Cy-rus! Cy-rus!"

As Cyrus began to distribute the shrimp to the ravenous masses, the rest of Group B joined the chorus, pumping their fists in the air and thanking him for his brave sacrifice. Cyrus grinned proudly, thrilled with his newfound fame. Andi might have made a valid point about how unfair it was that some people had been given more than others on that particular school day—but Cyrus had adjusted to that happening long ago. If he was being totally honest, he didn't entirely mind that the deck had finally been stacked in *his* favor. It was about freaking time!

Meanwhile, Andi watched Cyrus being showered with adoration and smiled. "I don't need a cheer," she said to herself. "It was enough that I blazed the trail."

● ● ●

Once everyone had gotten their fill of shrimp, Jonah's nose perked up and a huge grin spread across his face. "I smell something."

"Cookies," Buffy said, her eyes widening and her stomach still growling. After all, one bowl of shrimp only went so far with the malnourished Group B. "Freshly . . . baked . . . *cookies*!"

Buffy and Jonah beamed as they watched the cafeteria workers on the Group A side pull giant sheets of chocolate chip cookies out of an oven and set them on the counter to cool.

But then Jonah's smile faded. "We won't get any," he said with a sigh. "They'll go straight to Group A."

"No!" Buffy cried, finding her rebel spirit at last. "We can't let that happen!"

But the wheels were already turning in Andi's head. "Or maybe we can!" she pointed out, standing up and grinning.

Andi walked over to Cyrus and pulled him up from his seat. "Cyrus, I need you!"

Cyrus insisted he was too full of shrimp to move, but Andi wouldn't take no for an answer. As Buffy and Jonah encouraged their friends to go for it, Andi dragged Cyrus over to the kitchen on the Group A side, where the cookies were still sitting out on trays, cooling.

"Hi, we're from Group A!" Andi smiled at the women behind the counter as she grabbed two huge trays of cookies, and Cyrus did the same. "The smell was driving us crazy; we're just going to take these out for you."

Andi quickly spun around with her trays and motioned for Cyrus to follow her.

"Group A forever!" Cyrus yelled at the cafeteria workers as he joined Andi.

When they got a little distance from the window, they turned to each other and Andi shouted, "Run!"

At first, Cyrus looked worried. "Me? Run?" But then he remembered his triumphant dodgeball turn in gym class earlier that day. "Oh, right, I'm an athlete now!"

Cyrus and Andi bolted over to the Group B side of the cafeteria. But moments after they made it through the gate and set down the cookies, someone from Group A smelled the baked goods, leapt to his feet, pointed a finger at Andi and Cyrus, and screamed. It was Gus—the kid who had been so proud of solving the baby giraffe pop quiz in first period. When Andi and Cyrus turned and realized they'd been caught, Gus screamed even louder and proceeded to storm the gate. The dude was practically frothing at the mouth, like he was turning into some sort of brains-starved zombie.

Upon discovering what Gus already had, the rest of Group A jumped up and began to scream and wail, too. It was as if they hadn't eaten anything, let alone a full gourmet spread, in days, and just like Gus, they were all transforming into the walking—or more like sprinting—dead. Buffy and Jonah tried to hold the gate closed, but the kids from Group A were reaching over the top and wriggling their arms through every available space, pushing with all their might. It didn't take long for them to force the gate open. And when they did, nobody was safe from their ferocious attack.

Especially the baked goods.

CHAPTER 7

With cookies flying everywhere, Group A continued to attack Group B with all their might, committed to getting back what they believed was rightfully theirs. But Group B had had enough; they'd been kicked down and forced to accept that they were inferior to Group A for the better part of the day, and they weren't going to take it anymore. It was time to fight back, to question authority, to eat the cookies. *All* the cookies!

In the midst of the chaos, Gus, stumbling across the crumb-covered cafeteria floor, suddenly looked down at his chest and screamed even louder than before. On the upper right quadrant of his gray button-down shirt was something red and sticky.

"I've been hit! I've been hit!" Gus screeched in horror, his mouth gaping wide enough to reveal that most of the cookies he'd attempted to consume were stuck in his braces. He was even paler than usual and looked like he was about to faint at the sight of what he believed to be his own blood.

Buffy ran past him with fists full of her hard-won cookie contraband and assured him that it was just cocktail sauce.

Gus breathed a genuine sigh of relief.

Meanwhile, Cyrus was plucking cookies from the floor and shoving them into his mouth. "Five-second rule!" he shouted.

As kids continued to dive and lunge for the cookies, playing tug-of-war with the trays, Dr. Metcalf stepped into the frenzied crowd and blew a whistle. Finally, the screaming stopped . . . and the rest of the cookies dropped.

"Today's exercise is over!" the principal announced, looking around at the disheveled student body, along with the tables, benches, and floors of the cafeteria—every last inch covered in cookie debris. "There is no more Group A, and there is no more Group B." Then, noticing one long-haired girl in ripped jeans on the ground, and apparently unaware of Cyrus's prior offenses, he added, "And we're not eating cookies off the floor, Denise."

As the girl glanced up and rose to her feet, a mortified look on her chocolate-smeared face, everyone turned their attention to Dr. Metcalf, who asked, "Can anyone tell me the point of today's exercise?"

"It's about privilege," Buffy quickly responded as the principal walked past her. Clearly impressed, he turned and nodded, encouraging her to keep going.

"It's about one group thinking they deserve more than another . . ." Buffy's voice trailed off.

Again, Dr. Metcalf nodded, and then he turned to face the crowd of students who were gathered around. "Just because of the color . . . of their *wristband*," he concluded, looking pointedly—and even a bit sadly—into the faces of his students.

"But, uh, the people in Group A *were* better," Gus stammered.

Jonah grimaced as he shook his head and walked up to Gus, shooting daggers into his fogged-up, cookie-covered glasses. "Better at *what*?"

"Good question!" Dr. Metcalf pointed a finger at Jonah, who was posturing like he was about to take Gus down. The principal stepped between the two boys as he continued. "How did I decide who got to be in Group A?"

The students all looked at each other, dumb-founded. Even Buffy was stumped. But then Andi said, "It was completely random."

The principal smiled at her and then shook his head. *"Wrong."*

But Andi insisted that was all there was to it. "I mean, I don't know—you just said, 'Andi, Group A; Buffy, Group B.'"

Andi stared up at Dr. Metcalf, who nodded and told her to keep going.

"Keep going? Going *where*?" Andi spun around and wandered among her classmates, trying to recall the exact order in which they had been divided up that morning. "Cyrus, Group A. Denise, Group B." Andi looked around at the crowd. "Erin, Group A. Farrah, Group . . . B."

That was when it finally dawned on her. "You used the first letter of our names and just went back and forth!"

"Right," Dr. Metcalf said.

"So it was every other letter: A, C, E were in the A group; B, D, F were in the B group," Andi continued.

"And so on," the principal confirmed, his voice barely a whisper as he looked from one student to the next and spoke in the kindest voice any of them had ever heard him use since he'd started working there earlier in the school year. "Nobody here is better than anyone else."

Dr. Metcalf paused and let that sink in. As kids scrunched up their faces or turned to look at each other, some of them frowning, others with tears welling up in their eyes, he continued. "Nobody *anywhere* is better than anyone else."

Even the principal seemed like he might cry at that

point. He actually seemed nervous, his voice trembling as he concluded, "A lot of problems wouldn't even *be* problems if we all just accepted that simple fact. I hope you all learned that today. . . ."

Andi stared up at Dr. Metcalf and smiled. As crazy as the day had been—and as crazy as the principal often seemed—it had definitely offered lessons worth learning.

But then the principal continued. "Because the school board has hired a social sensitivity consultant and she's asked for your feedback."

Suddenly, the cafeteria erupted into a loud roar of complaints.

"What!" Andi demanded.

"You'll be hearing from my dry cleaner!" Gus shrieked.

"Can you explain that alphabet thing again?" another kid asked.

"Is that pop quiz still going to count?" Denise demanded.

"Are there more cookies?" Cyrus wondered.

But the principal just held up his hands defensively and started to back away. "Later. *In writing*," he said, making a beeline for the door. Before he made it all the way out of the cafeteria, though, he smiled and added, "And we need people to clean up. I choose . . . all of you!"

Realizing they were no longer divided, everyone started to laugh—especially Buffy and Andi, who gave each other a hug, and Jonah and Cyrus, who each wrapped an arm around the other. It felt good to be back on the same side again. *Really* good.

● ● ●

After school, Andi and Jonah were at the tables in front of the school, getting their wristbands cut off. As Jonah went to toss his away, Andi grabbed it.

"These aren't trash," she told him, setting her backpack down on the table and opening it up so she could put the wristband inside. She smiled sheepishly at the questioning look on his face and explained, "They're a carbon-neutral crafts project waiting to happen!"

Andi started picking up more of the discarded

wristbands, which were sitting on the table, and Jonah grabbed her bag and held it open—the gentlemanly thing to do—so she could put them inside.

"So what are you gonna make?" Jonah asked, almost like he was interviewing a celebrity whose work he'd always admired.

"Not sure." Andi shrugged and grabbed more wristbands. "Sometimes I go in without a plan, feel it out, and improvise. Like jazz—but way less boring . . . and with more washi tape." Noticing that Jonah was smiling at her, Andi smiled back and asked, "What?"

"You're so creative, and you're so smart," Jonah replied softly as they both swung their backpacks onto their shoulders. "I can't believe you figured out Metcalf's code."

"That was by accident," Andi pointed out, ever the picture of humility.

"Ah! You're even smart by accident!" Jonah grinned and bit down on his lower lip, then stared into Andi's eyes for what seemed like hours.

A little nervous laugh escaped Andi's lips. Then, before she could even comprehend what was happening,

Jonah reached for her hand. The second they made contact, it felt like there were a million tiny electrical currents buzzing through her fingertips.

Andi couldn't believe it. Jonah was holding her hand—and she was holding his! It had happened. It had finally happened!

"Sorry, sometimes my palms get sweaty," Jonah said, his cheeks flushing bright red as they continued to walk.

Andi giggled again. Should she tell him about hyperhidrosis? Nah. She didn't want to ruin the moment. And what a moment it was.

CHAPTER 8

When Andi got home, she was still walking on air, blissful to the point of being loopy.

"Heeeeeyyy," she said when she walked into the apartment and discovered Bex and Bowie sitting in the living room.

"Hey!" Bex and Bowie replied in unison, smiling at each other.

"How was your day?" Bex added, her nerves beginning to kick in when she realized that Andi was in an especially good mood.

At least she had Bowie there for moral support. He had promised he would help Bex break the awful news to Andi, and she could not have been more grateful to him for that.

"*Goooood.*" Andi started wriggling, almost dancing, and Bex's heart sank even deeper.

"Want to tell us what was so good about it?" Bex sucked in her breath, hoping Bowie was realizing the same thing she was—that Andi was beyond happy, and that there was no way they could tell her anything that might ruin what had clearly been a perfect day.

"*Noooooooo.*" Andi shook her head and marched straight for her bedroom, but Bowie grabbed her arm to stop her.

Bex knew he was only trying to help, but she still cringed. Did they really have to tell her then? Like, *right then*?

"Andi, sit down for a sec," Bowie said, guiding her toward the couch and sinking down onto the coffee table as Bex stood up. "We have something to tell you."

Andi glided over and plopped down on the sofa, then finally noticed the worried looks on Bex's and

Bowie's faces. She didn't want to ask, but she knew she had to. "What's . . . going on?"

Bowie hesitated and mashed his lips together. He glanced back at Bex and stood up, placing an arm gently around her shoulders. Bex looked up at him with nervous eyes, but Bowie whispered that she should just rip off the bandage—and at that point, she really didn't have a choice. So she swallowed hard and looked down at Andi.

After a few deep breaths, Bex finally said the words she had been hoping she would never have to say out loud: "Pops and CeCe are selling the house."

Andi's face froze, except for her mouth, which uttered the words "What?" "Why?" and "Where are they going?"

"Someplace smaller," Bowie interjected, doing his best to shrug it off, to make it seem like no big deal. "They don't need all the space."

"But . . . what about Andi Shack?" Andi leapt up from the couch, searching her parents' faces for something, anything, that would indicate they had a plan for saving her favorite place on the entire planet—that they knew how much it mattered to her. "What happens to Andi Shack?"

"Don't worry, we'll find room for your craft supplies," Bex said before realizing she sounded like an even more evil version of CeCe, if such a creature actually existed.

"Andi Shack is *not* just the place that I keep my glue gun!" Andi's voice was desperate, determined, angry—exactly how Bex's had sounded when she'd made a similar argument to CeCe earlier that day.

"We know that," Bowie told her, still trying to keep up the *everything's cool* act.

"No, you don't! You guys *just* showed up! Andi Shack has been there for my whole life!" Andi could feel tears beginning to sting her eyes now, and she didn't even care that she was saying hurtful things she might regret later. All she knew was that she could barely breathe, that she was on the verge of suffocating, and that it felt like her entire world was crumbling beneath her feet.

"We'll figure something else out," Bowie said, but this time he sounded a bit more worried .... desperate, even. This wasn't going nearly as well as he had hoped. Bex had been right. Andi was already crushed, and he wasn't so sure he could protect her after all.

"No, we won't! There's nothing else like it!" Then, without even realizing what she was saying, Andi glared at Bex and added, "I wish we'd never left home!"

It was exactly as Bex had feared. Andi blamed her—*of course* she blamed her. Worse still, there was a good chance that she might never forgive her.

Moments later, Andi was out on the sidewalk, running back to her old house, leaving Bowie and Bex to stare at each other, completely defeated. With her cheeks now wet with tears, Andi leapt over the shrubs in front of the house and headed straight for Andi Shack. Once inside, she spun around to look at the walls, taking in her supplies and all the things she'd made. It had always been the one place that made her feel better no matter how crazy life got. But where would she go to feel better after CeCe and Pops sold the house?

As Andi collapsed onto the floor, her thoughts drifted back to how happy she'd been less than an hour before—when Jonah had told her how creative and smart she was, and finally held her hand. But none of that mattered now. None of it was enough to stop the aching in her chest. Andi had just collected all those wristbands, planned on making something amazing with them. But what could she possibly make if she had no place to create? How could she be happy about anything ever again if she didn't have Andi Shack?

Suddenly, the best afternoon of her life had turned into the worst. And she couldn't help feeling like Bex was at least partly—if not entirely—to blame.

PART
TWO

CHAPTER 1

The world as Andi knew it was coming to an end. Oh, it had nothing to do with CeCe and Pops selling the house and her losing Andi Shack in that potentially devastating real estate deal. As it turned out, Andi had saved the world—or, at least, *her* world—by simply proposing that she spend a lot more time back at the old house. It was a solution that made CeCe, Pops, *and* Andi happier than any of them could have imagined.

But in the weeks since, something else had pulled the rug out from beneath Andi's very existence: Buffy's mom, who was in the military, had been assigned to work in Phoenix—so, exactly as the fortune teller at

Cyrus's Bar Mitzvah had predicted, Buffy would soon be leaving town. For good.

In spite of all of Andi's best efforts to find a way to keep Buffy in Shadyside, including having her move into Andi's old bedroom at CeCe and Pops's house, nothing had worked. The simple reality was that as much as Buffy's mom understood her daughter's reasons for wanting to stay put—a kid her age needed some stability, especially when it came to school and friends—she also couldn't bear the thought of missing more of Buffy's life than she already had during so many previous deployments.

As it turned out, Buffy felt the same way. She loved her friends and dreaded the thought of leaving them, and she shuddered to think how the basketball team would survive without her . . . or, really, how the entire academic foundation of Jefferson Middle School might collapse without her there. But she wanted to be with her mom more than anything, and who could blame her? Definitely not Andi. So now, with just seven days left to be together, Andi, Buffy, and Cyrus were desperate to squeeze a little bit of friendship magic out of every last remaining second.

"Come on, guys, *think*!" Andi shot a pleading look at Buffy and Cyrus, who were sitting on the olive-green velvet sofa in Bex and Andi's apartment. "We only have a week left with each other."

"I *know*." Buffy sighed and hugged an embroidered pink pillow to her chest. "I don't *want* to think about it."

"It's the world's saddest countdown . . . and at the end, we launch Buffy," Cyrus said softly. Unlike Buffy, who sat cross-legged, he was stretched out with his stripy-socked feet on the coffee table, and his dark wavy hair wasn't nearly as styled as usual. In fact, it was almost *messy*, like he'd rolled out of bed and headed over to Andi and Bex's apartment without even looking in the mirror. Which was a completely un-Cyrus-like move. Wasn't he the one who had dubbed the three of them the "Good Hair Crew" a few months earlier?

Truth be told, though, Andi could understand why Cyrus was having a bad hair day. She hadn't felt much like dealing with personal hygiene, either—let alone anything else—since finding out that Buffy was moving away. Still, she had somehow managed to shower and run a bit of product through her dark pixie cut before her friends came over that morning. She'd even put on one of her favorite new shirts—at first, it looked like a plain white tee with a few little red accents, but it was actually designed to look like a three-of-hearts playing card. Maybe she was being weirdly sentimental, but the moment Andi saw it, she decided that the three of hearts symbolized her, Buffy, and Cyrus.

But if they were going to have to be separated, Andi was determined to make every last day before that happened epic—a fact that she pointed out to Buffy and Cyrus as she leaned forward in her chair. "We don't want to waste the little time we have left just doing the same thing we always do," Andi continued.

She knew she didn't need to spell it out for her friends, and if she was being completely honest, "the same thing we always do" was one of the *many* things Andi was going to miss most after Buffy left. But just

in case they didn't know what she meant, ~~she rolled~~
her eyes and drove her point home: "Sitting at The
Spoon and having baby taters."

Buffy nodded and hugged the pillow tighter as she
readjusted her position on the couch. "But it's *hard* to
think of an epic day," she lamented. "The best days
we've ever spent together have just kind of happened
by accident."

Andi's eyes grew wide, and she stood up. "That's it!"

"What is?" Buffy glanced at Cyrus, wondering if
he knew what Andi was talking about. Of course, he
didn't—but that was fine. Buffy could see that Andi
was about to go on one of her hyper-enthusiastic rolls.
When the girl had an idea, she *really* had an idea, and
she committed to it 110 percent. It was one of about a
million things that Buffy loved, and would miss, about
her best friend.

"You can't just create an epic day out of thin air,"
Andi explained, getting more excited by the second.
"So let's *re-create* one we already had. Our Perfect
Day!"

"Great idea!" Cyrus sat up, almost as excited as Andi, but then sank back into the couch cushions, more confused than enthused. "What day was that again?"

Buffy laughed as she watched Andi rack her brain, trying to remember the best day they'd ever had together. Then . . . in three, two, one . . . it finally came to her.

"Oh!" Andi's mouth dropped open. "Remember when we went on that bike ride a few years ago? It was the day we discovered the Alpine Slide."

"Ohhh, the Alpine Slide!" Buffy nodded, a giant smile spreading across her face.

Cyrus got a blissed-out, faraway look in his eyes as he climbed aboard the memory train—or, rather, memory *slide*. "And on the way, we found that place with the hot apple cider and the pumpkin donuts!" he reminded them.

"The pumpkin donuts!" Buffy gurgled. She was practically drooling, like she could already taste them.

"Let's do it again! Today!" Andi proposed.

"Yes!" Buffy agreed as Bex walked into the living room with a plate of pizza pockets.

"Do what again?" Bex asked, waving the plate over their heads.

Buffy and Andi reached for the pizza pockets, but Bex quickly shifted the plate out of their reach and set it down on the coffee table. "Wait a second before you eat these," Bex said. "They're either still very hot or still need to thaw."

But Andi had no interest in discussing what was very likely still-frozen food. She turned to Bex and sucked in her breath before making her big announcement. "Get this: *we* are going to re-create our Perfect Day!"

"Oh." Bex leaned awkwardly against the sofa, unable to muster the slightest bit of enthusiasm.

"*Oh?* That's all my brilliant idea gets is 'oh'?" Andi scowled at Bex, who looked almost as scruffy as Cyrus in her old plaid flannel shirt and ripped jeans, with her dark hair piled messily on top of her head. The just-rolled-out-of-bed thing was one of her classic looks, and somehow, she always managed to make it work. She *always* looked so cool—and, more than that, she *was* so cool. She'd been on so many incredible adventures. So of course Andi had been hoping that Bex would hear her plan for the day and confirm that Andi was equally cool—that the Andi apple hadn't fallen far from the Bex tree.

Alas, Bex looked apologetically from Andi to Buffy to Cyrus before trying to explain, as gently as possible: "Well . . . in my experience, you *can't* re-create the perfect day."

Andi wasn't sure she wanted Bex to answer, but against her better judgment, she asked why not.

"I guess it's just never as good as the memory," Bex offered, still sort of developing the theory as she spoke. "It's like . . . bringing home leftovers. You're never going to love it as much as you did at the restaurant. It's always just going to be . . . reheated meat."

Andi scowled, because first of all, *ew*—"reheated meat" sounded positively disgusting—and second of all, there was no way she and her friends could ever be disappointed by the Alpine Slide or those insanely delicious pumpkin donuts.

"No!" Andi insisted, leaping to her feet and staring Bex down. "You're wrong. You *have* to be. We have *not* had our last great day together." Andi turned to Buffy and Cyrus, snapping back into motivational speaker mode. "Come on, guys, we can do this! Today will *not* be reheated meat!"

Andi watched as Cyrus and Buffy exchanged smiles.

"It's a weird rallying cry," Cyrus said, before getting up from the couch—and Andi had to confess, he was totally right. "But . . . I'm on board!"

"Me too!" Buffy grinned and leapt up from the couch as well.

So just like that, they had a plan. Now all they had to do was grab their bikes and make it happen!

CHAPTER 2

Later that morning, after an agonizing hour or two of digging their childhood bikes out of their families' garages, Andi and her friends met up and headed down Main Street, accompanied by the grating sound of squeaking tires and clunking metal.

Andi glanced at Cyrus's black BMX bike and then at Buffy's hot-pink five-speed and realized that even though Cyrus's front tire was hanging from the handlebars and Buffy's ride was covered in dust and cobwebs, Andi's was easily the oldest of them all—a lime-green dinosaur bike with a banana seat and a wicker basket. But that was because it had never been Andi's bike to begin with; it had belonged to Bex.

As the three of them creaked to a stop beneath the striped canopy of Red Rooster Records, they regarded each other's bikes and Andi acknowledged what they were all thinking, while still trying to remain upbeat: "Okay, so our plan has a hiccup. Three . . . very old . . . *rusty* hiccups."

Buffy nodded, her dark eyes full of an uncharacteristic amount of concern. "I haven't ridden my bike in years," she admitted with a gulp.

"Me neither," Cyrus said, glancing over at Andi's bike. "But at least mine didn't have to time-travel here from the sixties."

"I'm using Bex's old bike because I sold mine," Andi pointed out defensively. Surely Buffy and Cyrus hadn't forgotten—trading in her ten-speed, along with forking over at least a years' worth of cat-sitting money, to get a shiny yellow electric scooter had been part of her big plan to become more adventurous and rebellious when she'd turned thirteen. "But it's still totally rideable."

Andi tried to ring the rusty old bell, but the moment she touched it, it fell off the handlebar and clunked sadly on the sidewalk, breaking into at least a dozen pieces. Andi looked back at her friends, trying to appear less uneasy than she felt. They *had* to find a way to make her plan work—but how were they going to do that if their bikes weren't even in riding condition?

● ● ●

An hour or so later, Andi, Buffy, and Cyrus stood outside of a big trailer emblazoned with the words WHEEL WORKS MOBILE REPAIR SHOP and stared down in awe of their newly spruced-up bikes.

"If I had known there was a place that would clean and service your bike for you, I would have been riding mine all the time," Cyrus said, putting on his black bicycle helmet.

Buffy smirked and set a hand on Cyrus's shoulder. "No, you wouldn't."

Cyrus had to agree as he stared down at the ground. "Nah, I wouldn't."

Having finished paying for the repairs, Bex strolled over and squatted down next to her old bike, gripping one of the handlebars like she was squeezing the hand of a long-lost pal. "Aw! It's been a while since old Skidboot looked this good!"

Andi stifled a laugh. "Skidboot? You *named* your bike?"

Bex's eyes widened in protective horror. "Shhh," she whispered to Andi while stroking the green banana seat lovingly. "You're hurting her feelings."

Cyrus raised his eyebrows at Bex and tilted his head to the side, mildly amused at what he had previously presumed to be a gender-neutral vehicle. "Skidboot's a girl?"

Realizing Andi and her friends were never going to understand, Bex stood up and changed the subject to one that had been plaguing her ever since Andi had proposed this little adventure. If she was totally honest with herself, Bex was a bit nervous about letting Andi make this trip with her friends. After all, they were barely in their teens! And getting to the Alpine Slide was going to involve traversing steep hills, rickety bridges, and sketchy dirt roads. Thinking about Andi out there, all alone—or, okay, with Buffy and Cyrus—was bringing out all of Bex's protective maternal instincts. It was one of the first times in her life that she could kind of relate to what CeCe must have gone through whenever Bex had taken off—or, at least, whenever she'd *known* about Bex taking off.

"Okay, so you all have your helmets . . . Do you have your phones?" Bex asked, sounding a lot more panicked than she'd intended. "And two forms of ID?"

"Mom! Stop being such a . . . *mom*," Andi groaned before turning to Buffy and Cyrus and wiggling her shoulders excitedly. "Okay, who's ready for Perfect Day 2.0?"

But Bex wasn't finished. "Oh—and I'll have my phone right next to me at all times if you need anything."

"Thanks, but we won't," Andi retorted, turning to her friends again and flashing a huge smile. "First stop, pumpkin donuts!"

As they all hopped onto their bikes, Buffy threw down one of her usual challenges and shouted out, "Last one there buys the cider!"

So while Bex watched her only daughter hit the road, she couldn't help feeling like she was watching Andi learn to ride a bike for the very first time—and not just because she'd missed that milestone moment when it had occurred so many years ago. As Andi and her friends began pumping their pedals as hard as they could, they should have been speeding off, but instead it was more like they were wobbling off. Sure, their bikes were no longer rusty . . . but their riding skills were another matter.

"Whoa!" Cyrus muttered, jerking his handlebars from side to side and nearly falling off. "Okay, definitely been a while. I forgot how to do this."

"Huh," Buffy said, wincing. But even though she, too, was shaky and struggling to get the hang of it, she couldn't let the opportunity to make a clever joke pass her by. "I guess riding a bike . . . *isn't* 'like riding a bike.'"

Normally, Andi would have laughed, but she was having a tough time riding in a straight line as well. Still, she was determined to make it work. "Don't read into this!" she shouted back to Bex, who was still watching the world's most tragic bike race with a look of dread.

"Trying not to!" Bex called back, shoving her hands into the back pockets of her distressed jeans, her heart skipping another beat as Andi hit a bump and visions of broken limbs flashed through Bex's mind.

So maybe Perfect Day 2.0 hadn't started off *exactly* like the original Perfect Day, but Andi was certain that she and her friends would ultimately disprove Bex's "reheated meat" theory. She knew that once they got to the cider stand, everything really would be perfect. They just needed to relearn to ride their bikes first.

CHAPTER 3

Sure enough, after they'd been pedaling for a while, Andi and her friends finally found their bicycling groove—or, at least, Andi and Buffy did. As they became more and more comfortable winding along the dusty dirt roads, pedaling as hard as they could, the race was back on!

First Andi took the lead, but then Buffy nearly crashed into her as they crossed a bridge and managed to pull ahead. All the while, Cyrus struggled to keep up with them, nearly losing control every time he hit the tiniest pebble or bump, his legs feeling more like lead the longer he tried to pedal. Eventually, when they came to a flat, paved bike path running alongside a grassy park, Andi and Buffy doubled back to make sure he was okay. After getting *some* assurance that he was, and that they should go on ahead without him, the girls agreed and merged back onto the final dirt road that would take them to the cider stand at last.

When Andi and Buffy got to their destination, it was every bit as perfect as they remembered: a quaint cabin-like structure with barrels full of apples on the front porch in every imaginable variety—bright red McIntosh, green Granny Smith, gorgeous Golden Delicious. There were also fairy lights hanging from the roof, glass jugs full of cider set up in a tall wooden display case, and a giant red plastic apple hanging beneath a green sign that read NEWTON'S CIDER & DONUTS. Then Andi saw the best part of all—the octagonal wooden picnic table where she, Buffy, and Cyrus had taken their first bites of the most delicious pumpkin donuts they'd ever tasted.

After she and Buffy locked up their bikes and stood around for what felt like an hour, Andi began to wonder what was taking Cyrus so long. She stared over at the bike path, searching through the trees for him.

"Do you see him?" Andi asked Buffy, who was also looking off into the distance.

"Not yet," Buffy said, her voice shaking a bit.

"You think we need to worry about him?" Andi frowned.

Buffy nodded. "Always."

As the girls giggled nervously, Cyrus finally appeared—still a little wobbly, but making solid progress across the last wooden bridge.

"Here he comes," Buffy said, relieved.

Finally, accompanied by a whole lot of huffing and puffing, Cyrus made it to the bike rack, where Andi and Buffy were waiting for him. "Sorry," he said, gasping for air. "My bike only has one gear."

"Um, no it doesn't," Buffy replied, gesturing at his handlebar, where gears one through six were clearly marked. "Your shifter's right there."

Cyrus's jaw dropped as he examined the dial. "Okay," he said with a frustrated sigh, "that information might have been more helpful, like, three quarters of a mile ago."

Andi and Buffy laughed, and then Andi's eyes

widened as she sniffed the air. "Guys . . ." she gasped blissfully, "do you smell what I smell?"

Buffy and Cyrus closed their eyes and inhaled deeply.

"Pumpkin donuts!" Cyrus cheered.

"Let's do this!" Buffy smiled, and she and Andi eagerly took off for the cider stand.

"Um—hello, a little help?" Cyrus scowled, guiding his bike into the rack and struggling to get it locked up while shouting out to the girls, "At least get me a cider!"

The moment they got inside Newton's, Andi knew that Perfect Day 2.0 was totally happening . . . and there was no reheated meat in sight. Instead, they sampled every last kind of candy on display in the shop and checked out the tacky souvenirs. The best ones were the tiny personalized license plates—mostly because they couldn't find any of their names, so they instead decided to purchase the closest available options. That meant that Andi got to be Randy, Buffy was Buddy, and Cyrus became Cyril. They even got one for Bex, who would thereafter be known as Jeff.

As they paid for their new identities, the three friends couldn't stop laughing—so side-splittingly hard that tears rolled down their cheeks. Andi honestly couldn't remember the last time that had happened. She was so glad they'd made this trip! And then, once they'd finally recovered from their hysterics, they got their cider and donuts and settled in at the picnic table on the front porch.

"This hot apple cider is even *better* than I remembered it," Buffy said, sighing happily after taking a sip.

"Right?" Andi agreed, staring adoringly at the brown paper cup. "It's like they captured my childhood, added cinnamon, and put it in a biodegradable cup."

Buffy laughed at her always eco-conscious friend and then admitted, "I think I want another pumpkin donut."

"Me too!" Cyrus gushed, his dark eyes lighting up as he grabbed his half-eaten donut and carefully studied its delicately glazed surface. "I wonder who created pumpkin spice? Because I would like to shake the hand of the person who managed to *improve sugar!*"

Buffy nodded and scrunched up her nose, legitimately baffled as her thoughts drifted back to the original Perfect Day that had inspired this one. "The real question is, why did we wait five years to come back here?"

"Yeah," Cyrus agreed, casting a look of reverence in Andi's direction. "This was the perfect idea."

As Andi flashed a victorious smile, her phone rang. Glancing at the screen, she discovered it was Bex and put it on speaker, then set it in the middle of the table. She couldn't *wait* to tell Bex how wrong she'd been about their ability to re-create their perfect day. "Checking up on us?" Andi asked, fighting the urge to roll her eyes at the phone.

"Nooo!" Bex insisted, although it was obvious from the concern in her voice that she was desperate for information that would put her fears to rest. "I just want to know where you are and how you're doing, which is totally different from checking up on you."

All three of them laughed and then Andi excitedly reported, "Everything's great!"

"The cider is fantastic!" Buffy chimed in.

"So are the donuts," Cyrus added.

Andi tried not to sound too boastful, but she couldn't help rubbing it in, just a tiny bit. "You might even say it's been a *perfect day* so far . . . ?"

"*Better* than perfect!" Buffy enthused.

"Per-*fect*-a-mundo!" Cyrus added with a wink.

That did it—Andi and her friends had put Bex's doubts to rest. Or, at least, the hint of relief in her voice suggested as much. "Sounds like you're having fun," Bex told them. "Carry on."

"Will do!" Andi replied, ending the call.

Then she, Buffy, and Cyrus headed back into the cider shop to get another round of donuts. Because as perfect as the day had already been, more sugar and spice would make it extra nice.

CHAPTER 4

Back in the center of town, Bowie was checking out strings in his favorite guitar shop when he heard someone barrel through the door. He spun around to discover Jonah nearly tripping over the racks of used records before stumbling backward. Bowie narrowed his eyes, observing the kid for a few more seconds. He was breathing hard and so sweaty his brown hair was matted to his forehead. Bowie frowned. Jonah seemed completely freaked out about something—it was almost as if he'd seen a ghost. Or, from the way he was panting, like he'd been *chased* by a ghost.

"Hey, Jonah!" Bowie called out, but Jonah apparently didn't hear him. So Bowie shouted his name a bit louder, which seemed to startle him—his blue eyes grew wide and even more scared, and when he blinked in Bowie's direction, it was almost as if he didn't recognize him. Bowie was really worried now. He walked over and asked if Jonah was okay.

Jonah nodded and tried to conceal his angst. "I-I just . . . ran here is all." He glanced around the shop, looking almost confused as to how he'd wound up there, still struggling to catch his breath.

"You're good. Just breathe," Bowie advised, putting a reassuring hand on Jonah's shoulder. "Do you want some water?"

"No, I'll be fine in a second," Jonah insisted, but he didn't sound convinced.

"Why were you in such a hurry to get here?" Bowie asked.

"Um . . ." Jonah looked around the shop, still disoriented but trying to come up with a believable excuse. Noticing all the instruments hanging on the wall and sitting on stands around the room, it finally came to him. "To . . . to . . . buy a guitar! I needed to buy a guitar."

"I didn't know you played!" Bowie still sensed something else was going on with Jonah, but maybe talking music would help calm him down. It had always helped Bowie, anyway.

"I don't, um . . ." Jonah searched his mind for another plausible reason for being there. "I just . . . just . . . wanted to learn?"

"Oh, yeah?" Bowie nodded, encouraging Jonah to keep talking. "What inspired you?"

"Oh, you know . . . music!" Jonah flung his arms up in an exaggerated shrug and let out a little laugh. "Is there somewhere to sit down?" he added, glancing around the shop again.

Jonah felt a bit queasy as he observed the early afternoon light filtering through the blinds in the front window, causing shards of light to dance eerily across the mustard yellow walls and distort the images on the old concert posters. There was also a strange mural that Jonah couldn't quite make sense of—it was like a woman's face, but there were black vinyl records where her hair should have been. As his breathing finally started to slow, his vision got less blurry, enough for him to finally realize: the records *were* her hair! Or, at least, they were supposed to look like her hair. Or . . . something.

Jonah glanced up at Bowie, who had thankfully grabbed a wooden stool for him. "This is a big day," Bowie said, giving the stool an enthusiastic pat before heading over to pull an acoustic instrument down from the wall. He passed it to Jonah. "I remember when I got my first guitar. My dad taught me everything he knew."

"Was he a good musician?" Jonah asked distractedly as Bowie picked up a black acoustic guitar from a nearby stand.

"No, horrible," Bowie replied with a laugh. "He only knew three chords. But . . . he taught them to me, so they're still my favorites. Here, I'll show you."

With a faraway look in his eye, Bowie slowly placed his fingers on the strings, explaining as he went. "These three go there . . ." Bowie said, and Jonah copied what he was doing. "There you go!" Bowie nodded and strummed a chord. "That's a *D*."

Jonah strummed tentatively, looking up at Bowie for some reassurance.

Bowie nodded again and gave Jonah an encouraging laugh, then changed the position of Jonah's fingers on the frets and strings before strumming his own guitar. "Now, this is an *A*."

Jonah copied him perfectly.

"Then *G*," Bowie instructed.

Jonah replicated him again.

"Congratulations," Bowie said, waving a hand in the air with a flourish. "You now know the *best* three chords in the world."

A little laugh escaped Jonah's lips and he looked down at his hands, which he was relieved to discover were no longer shaking. "That is . . . kinda great."

"I can show you some more if you want," Bowie offered, happy to see that playing guitar did seem to be helping Jonah mellow out.

"Now? Will the store owner mind?" Jonah glanced around and realized they were practically alone, except for one or two guys hanging out by the register in the middle of the shop. He also realized how comfortable he was beginning to feel—focusing on playing guitar had definitely helped stop the room from spinning.

"Nah, he's my friend. We jam," Bowie replied, gesturing over to back of the shop, where there was a little coffee bar and open mic area. "I've performed here a bunch. You should come and check me out sometime."

"I will." Jonah smiled.

Bowie nodded. "Cool! So, ready for your next chord?"

"Bring it!" Jonah agreed, finally feeling almost completely at ease.

"All right!" Bowie curled his fingers around the neck of the guitar and started to strum.

So, just like that, Jonah's day went from completely frightening to kind of fantastic. In fact, as his guitar lesson with Bowie continued, he decided it was the closest thing he'd had to a perfect day in a long time.

CHAPTER 5

When they'd finally had their fill of pumpkin donuts, Andi and her friends were ready to move on to phase two of Perfect Day 2.0: an exhilarating ride down the Alpine Slide!

"Thanks again, Martha!" Cyrus shouted to the matronly woman behind the counter, before joining Andi and Buffy on the front steps of the cider stand. "One of these days I'll get that secret recipe from you!" Cyrus had done everything he could to charm her, but he still hadn't been able to make Martha tell him how she got those donuts to taste so good. Instead, she said he'd just have to keep coming back for more, which he had decided he would most definitely be doing.

"Oh! I hope the Alpine Slide still has those T-shirts," Buffy said, moving a hand dramatically in front of Andi's eyes as she described the shirt exactly as she remembered it: "*'Whoosh* you were here!'" Andi and Buffy laughed at the cheesy slogan, but then Buffy got serious, shaking Andi by the shoulders and insisting, "I *need* one!"

Before they could head for their bikes, though, Cyrus ran by, nearly knocking Buffy and Andi over as he ducked and waved his hands around in a panic. "Go away, bee!" he screamed, swatting the air. "I can't get stung!"

"Are you allergic?" Andi watched with a mixture of amusement and concern as Cyrus continued his efforts to evade the flying insect.

"No!" Cyrus called back to her. "I just suffer from hating things that hurt really bad."

Andi and Buffy laughed, and Cyrus finally stopped flailing around—not because the bee had disappeared, but because something else had. As Andi and Buffy followed Cyrus's line of sight, they discovered two broken locks dangling from the bike rack, along with Skidboot—the lone two-wheeled survivor.

"Someone stole my bike!" Cyrus gasped.

"Someone stole *my* bike!" Buffy added.

"Mine's still here," Andi said, relieved at first—but then, as the gravity of what had happened to Buffy and Cyrus sank in, she turned to face her friends. "But . . . someone stole *your* bikes."

Andi staggered over to the rack and grabbed the green plastic-encased chain that was supposed to have kept Buffy's bike safe. Someone had cut straight through it. Andi's heart sank. How was she going to salvage their perfect day when someone had violated her best friends this way?

"Let's just call Bex, ask her to pick us up," Buffy proposed as the three friends stood there by Skidboot and the broken locks. "*She'll* take us to the slide, I can get my T-shirt—"

"No!" Andi interrupted, staring down at the remains

of Buffy's chain and shaking it in protest. "That's not our day. We're re-creating our day!"

"We're already in new territory," Cyrus pointed out, his voice shaking.

"We can still get back on track," Andi insisted, pasting a less-than-convincing smile on her face.

"How?" Buffy scowled.

Andi's face fell, and she sucked in her breath. Was Buffy right? Should they just call Bex? *No!* Andi wasn't going to admit defeat. She would *not* give Bex the satisfaction of being right—of predicting that Perfect Day 2.0 would be as disappointing as reheated meat! Andi spun around and looked at Bex's old bike—the banana seat, the high handlebars. It could totally work!

"*This* is kind of roomy," she told her friends, flashing a slightly more authentic smile as she wrapped her fingers around one of Skidboot's white handlebar grips. "I bet we can all fit."

The look on Buffy's face suggested she was far from persuaded. "And ride it all the way to the slide?" She shot a *you-cannot-be-serious* sideways glance at Andi.

"We should . . . um . . . at least try!" Andi clapped her hands, mustering *almost* enough enthusiasm for the three of them.

"I call basket," Cyrus said with a shrug. At least he was *sort of* meeting Andi halfway on the eagerness front.

Although Buffy still felt hesitant, she also knew she was outnumbered—and, besides, she wasn't one to give up without a fight. That said, the moment they all climbed on the bike, Andi could barely keep it balanced with Buffy in front of her on the banana seat and Cyrus looking nervous and wobbly on the basket.

"Anyone want to trade?" Cyrus stammered, clutching the handlebars behind him so tightly that his knuckles turned even paler than the rest of him. "I'm sorry I called basket!"

Buffy ignored the request and prepared to start pedaling. "Okay, ready?" she asked, briefly squeezing her eyes closed and shaking her head before taking a deep breath. "Here we go. One . . . two . . ."

But Buffy didn't even make it to the count of three

before Andi leapt from the seat and Cyrus bailed from the basket.

"Nope," Andi yelled.

"Never gonna happen," Buffy had to agree.

"We are not these kids," Cyrus concluded.

Andi puffed out her lower lip. Now what? She could already hear Bex saying, *I told you so.*

No! the voice in her head repeated. Maybe they weren't the kids who could all fit on an ancient bike, but they also weren't the kids who would let one tiny obstacle—or even two big stolen obstacles—get in the way of re-creating their perfect day.

● ● ●

About an hour later, the three friends were walking along the dirt road that would lead them to the Alpine Slide. As leaves fell from the trees overhead and carpeted the ground, Andi wearily pushed Skidboot with Buffy walking next to her and Cyrus lagging several yards behind.

"How far have we gone?" Cyrus called out.

"We're almost to the slide," Andi assured him.

"Are you lying to me?" Cyrus asked.

"Yes," Andi admitted.

"Thank you," Cyrus replied, looking down at the ground. "At least I wore my adventure shoes."

"You have *adventure* shoes?" Buffy smirked as she and Andi both glanced back at Cyrus and smiled.

Cyrus shrugged. "They don't get out much." But then, hearing something buzzing around, Cyrus screamed and raced ahead of Buffy and Andi. "The bee! He followed me!"

"He?" Andi asked. "How do you know it's the same one?"

"Trust me, it's him—bees won't *ever* leave me alone," Cyrus insisted as he ducked and screamed yet still managed to explain. "My bubbe says it's because I have sweet blood . . . but my doctor says it's because I sweat more than most boys."

Hearing another buzzing noise and now convinced the bee was about to go in for the kill, Cyrus screamed even louder and took off running faster than he had ever run in his life.

"Serpentine! Serpentine!" Buffy shouted. It was an

obscure reference to a hilarious old movie, but thankfully Cyrus got it and began to run in an evasive zigzag pattern. Until, that is, one of his feet sank into a deep mud puddle that had been concealed beneath all the fallen leaves on the dirt road.

Cyrus's screams echoed through the trees as his entire leg disappeared into the ground. "Help! I'm stuck!"

In almost as much of a panic, Andi and Buffy abandoned Skidboot and rushed over to help Cyrus. They each grabbed him by an arm and began to drag him out, but he went completely limp, making it ten times harder for them to move him.

"Cyrus, you could help a little," Buffy muttered, mud flying everywhere as she struggled to save him.

When Buffy and Andi finally did manage to get Cyrus back on his feet, Andi looked down and noticed something was missing. *Again.* "Where is your shoe?" she asked Cyrus.

Cyrus shook his head, defeated. "It belongs to the quicksand now."

Buffy rolled her eyes. "Oh, for Pete's sake." Then

she plunged her hand into the mud all the way to the elbow, feeling all around before finally pulling it back out, her arm dripping in slop, with no shoe to be found. "It's gone. Like, literally disappeared." She stood up and stared into Cyrus's eyes like she was in the middle of an *Unsolved Mysteries* TV marathon. "*How* do these things happen to you?"

"If I knew . . ." Cyrus frowned. "Well, for one, I'd still have a shoe."

Buffy couldn't help laughing, but Andi was starting to worry. "Now how are you going to walk?" Andi asked.

"I guess someone's just going to have to give me a piggyback ride," Cyrus quipped, choking out *"Buffy"* under his breath. "Or use the fireman's carry. I'm not picky."

Buffy shook her head and smirked. "Yeah, I'm not doing that."

That was when the sound of a police siren echoed around them. They all spun around and, with jaws dropped, discovered a patrol car pulling up beside them.

"You guys okay?" a woman in a light brown deputy's uniform and hat asked, stepping out of the vehicle with a look of motherly concern on her face. "Need a ride somewhere?"

"Yes! You're a lifesaver!" Buffy's face was positively glowing with renewed hope and Cyrus nodded giddily, while Andi offered a reluctant—albeit slightly relieved—smile.

Cyrus turned to Buffy. "Do you guys mind if I'm dropped off first?" Then, looking at Andi, he pleaded his case: "I survived quicksand!" Finally, he looked at the deputy and began to shout his home address to her.

But before Cyrus could finish, Andi interrupted and called out, "To the Alpine Slide!"

The officer looked surprised, especially considering the three of them were completely covered in mud. Still, much to Andi's delight, she agreed and told them to come on.

"Thank you!" Andi smiled, grabbing Buffy's arm so she could help her retrieve Skidboot from the side of the road and load her into the back of the patrol car.

Andi could tell that her friends were disappointed—that they wanted to go home, that they were completely over the whole notion of re-creating their perfect day. But there was no way she was going to allow this to be Buffy's final memory of their time together, let alone of their friendship. And it wasn't about proving Bex wrong. It was about proving that, as long as they were together, Andi, Buffy, and Cyrus could accomplish anything.

CHAPTER 6

Right around the same time that Andi, Buffy, and Cyrus were getting a lift from the local sheriff's deputy, Jonah was continuing to get his own version of a lift from Bowie. After flawlessly playing the basic three-chord tune that Bowie had just taught him, he looked up and smiled.

"Yeah!" Bowie nodded, his mouth dropping open as he marveled at Jonah's obvious natural talent. "You're *really* good."

Jonah rolled his eyes, assuming Bowie was just being nice. "Sure," he said with a shrug.

"No, seriously—I've never seen anyone pick up chords that fast," Bowie insisted, thinking back on his own early experiences with learning to play and how much of a struggle it had been for him. *Man!* He'd had to work so hard to get the fingering just right. It had taken Bowie *weeks* to get as good as Jonah had already gotten in under an hour.

Jonah sighed, genuinely grateful. "Thanks. This was really fun." Then, realizing it was probably about time for him to head out, he glanced down at the guitar and asked, "Where should I put this?"

"You're not gonna buy it? But you came in to get a guitar . . . *right*?" Bowie narrowed his eyes and studied Jonah's face. Of course, he'd already realized that Jonah hadn't really come into the shop to buy a guitar—but now that he'd witnessed the kid's incredible raw talent, he was hoping he might actually go through with the purchase. Especially considering how it seemed to have helped him get over whatever had been bothering him when he'd first stumbled in.

Realizing he'd been caught in a lie, Jonah frowned and shifted his eyes to the floor. How was he going to explain this one away? Seeing how flustered Jonah was becoming, Bowie asked, as gently as possible, what was going on with him.

"Nothing," Jonah replied, trying to smile, his voice barely a whisper as he bit down on his lower lip. "It's just . . . sometimes I get kinda stressed and I can't catch my breath. No big deal."

Bowie nodded—he had several friends who had described similar experiences to him through the years. "Jonah, that kind of sounds like a panic attack," Bowie pointed out with paternal concern.

"Yeah, that's what Cyrus's dad called it, too," Jonah admitted.

"And he's a doctor!" Bowie was relieved—at least Jonah was getting some kind of professional help. "That's great that you're seeing a doctor."

"I'm not." Jonah shook his head and exhaled loudly. How had he gotten himself into this mess? What was he doing there, opening up about all his problems . . . and to *Andi's dad*, no less? "He was just there, the way you were just here. I really don't want to keep having them . . . but I guess it doesn't matter what I want."

Bowie pressed his lips together and searched for the right words. He wanted to reassure Jonah, to let him know that he didn't need to feel alone in what he was going through. "If there's anything I can do—"

Jonah's face brightened slightly. He was sort of afraid to ask, but he also felt like he had to. "Yeah, there is," he said slowly, his blue eyes pleading with Bowie as he tried to conceal the desperation in his voice. "Don't tell Andi?"

"I won't," Bowie assured him with an empathetic pout. "I think she'd understand, but I won't."

Jonah grinned, relieved. "Thanks."

He was about to get up and leave, but before he could, Bowie stopped him. "Jonah, I know this was a weird way to discover it, but you've got a real talent for playing guitar."

Once again, in spite of the stressful conversation he'd just had with Bowie, Jonah felt like all his worries were melting away. "Well," he acknowledged with a sheepish grin, "I know it's really calmed me down."

"So, maybe you should think about playing more," Bowie proposed. "I can give you lessons!"

Jonah nodded. "I'll think about it. Thanks."

Bowie smiled and nodded back. "Yeah, man."

Then, as they bumped their fists together, it was as if they were making a pact to crush Jonah's anxiety . . . together. And for the first time since he'd started having panic attacks, Jonah realized that he might have more power over the situation than he'd thought—that maybe, eventually, everything would turn out okay. But he also knew he might not be able to do it by himself.

He now knew that for things to get easier, he would probably need to ask someone for help. He just hadn't realized that someone might be Bowie . . . or a guitar. But at least things were looking up. Things were *definitely* looking up.

CHAPTER 7

Things were starting to look up for Andi, Buffy, and Cyrus, too. After loading Skidboot and their bags into the back of the patrol car, and with Cyrus already in the front passenger seat, Andi and Buffy climbed into the back seat of the vehicle.

"Okay, ready!" Andi told the deputy, eager to get to the Alpine Slide and erase any hint of Perfect Day 2.0 being anything less than . . . perfect.

But then Buffy looked out the window and did a double take, realizing there were two teenagers riding along the dirt road on bikes that looked *extremely* familiar.

"You guys, look!" Buffy shouted. "Our bikes!"

"Deputy Bartlett," Cyrus chimed in, somehow maintaining a completely calm demeanor as he turned to look at the officer, "we'd like to report a crime."

"Those bikes are ours!" Buffy added, eyes lighting up and a hopeful smile crossing her lips. "Can you arrest them?"

"Probably not," the officer replied somewhat wearily. "But I can stop them."

Deputy Bartlett moved to turn her keys in the ignition, but stopped short when a call came in over the radio: *Unit Forty-Nine from dispatch, could you divert to a stolen car in progress at Seventh and Main? Respond code three.*

Deputy Bartlett spoke back into the handset: "Dispatch from Unit Forty-Nine, I'll be ten-seventy-six to that location." Then, turning to Andi, Buffy, and Cyrus, she added, "Sorry, guys. I'm going to need to drop you off."

Andi's face fell. She couldn't believe it! How was a stolen car more important than Buffy and Cyrus's stolen bikes—and, on an even more pressing note, how were they going to get to the Alpine Slide if Deputy Bartlett didn't take them there?

"Buckle up," the officer added, sending Andi's heart sinking even deeper than Cyrus's foot in a mud puddle.

"Can we turn on the siren?" Cyrus asked excitedly.

"No," Deputy Bartlett snapped.

● ● ●

Moments later, back in front of the cider stand, Andi, Buffy, and Cyrus stared sadly after the patrol car as it took off, sirens blaring. The three friends shivered in their mud-covered coats—partly because it was getting late and the skies were growing dark and cloudy, but mostly because Deputy Bartlett had let them down.

"Well, that's upsetting," Cyrus groused, watching the red lights flashing in the distance. "She'll turn on the siren for *them*, but not for *us*?"

"You know what's even more upsetting?" Buffy widened her eyes, which were still fixated on the rapidly departing vehicle. "We left our bike and backpacks in her trunk."

They all gasped, then started running after the patrol car screaming "STOP!"—even though the vehicle was already long gone.

Finally, they slowed to a halt, defeated.

"My phone was in my bag," Andi said, tears beginning to sting her eyes.

Buffy patted at the pockets of her puffy coat and panicked. "Mine too!"

"Luckily, I still have mine." Cyrus reached into the front pocket of his jeans and handed his phone to Buffy, who laughed happily . . . until she looked down at the screen.

"You're only at two percent!" Buffy reported.

"I took a lot of selfies in the police car," Cyrus explained with an innocent shrug.

Andi widened her eyes at Buffy. "Turn it off!" she commanded. "Turn. It. Off."

"We have enough for one call," Buffy insisted, holding the phone out to Andi. "Call Bex. Tell her to come pick us up."

"She's going to say, 'I told you so,'" Andi complained.

"She *did* tell us so," Buffy pointed out, pushing the phone toward Andi again.

Andi reluctantly took the phone, sucked in her breath, and pressed the button to call Bex, whose voice came through the speaker almost immediately.

"That was fast!" Bex said cheerily. "You're at the slide already?"

Andi gritted her teeth and replied wryly, "Yeah, we're real speed demons—"

"How was Skidboot? She give you any trouble?" Bex asked.

"No, Skidboot was great—" Andi said haltingly.

What are you doing? Buffy silently asked Andi with wide, shocked eyes, while Bex's voice continued to come through the speaker.

"Hey—I want to apologize for doubting you could pull this off," Bex said. "I know you guys. When you want to make something happen, it happens."

Andi, Buffy, and Cyrus all looked at each other sadly, knowing deep down that they were no longer the kids Bex was describing. Maybe they never had been.

Buffy nodded at Andi, pleading with her to tell Bex the truth—to ask her to pick them up. *Immediately.*

Andi stared back at her friend, visions of reheated meat making her stomach turn. But she knew what she had to do.

"Bex . . ." Andi began, as a little voice inside her head begged her not to give up. Not yet. Maybe it didn't feel like she, Buffy, and Cyrus were the kids who could make things happen right at that moment . . . but maybe they still *could* be those kids! So, even with Buffy's forceful glare fixed on her, Andi quickly changed her tune and spoke happily into the phone, "We're about to get on the chairlift, we gotta go—"

As Andi pressed the button to end the call, Cyrus screamed, "Nooo!" and Buffy shouted, "Bex!" while lunging for the phone.

"We're calling her back," Buffy insisted, grabbing the phone and pressing one button . . . and then another, the heat slowly rising to her cheeks as she dropped her arms to her sides and narrowed her eyes at Andi, furious. "It's out of power!"

Andi blinked apologetically at Buffy, unsure what to do next. But Cyrus had an idea. Spinning around and running toward the cider stand, he shouted, "They must have a phone in there! Heeeeelp!"

Buffy took off after Cyrus, while Andi followed slowly behind. When Cyrus and Buffy got to the door, however, they discovered a chalkboard sign that read CLOSED. Still, they began pounding on the door.

"Hello?" Cyrus shouted. "Anyone in there? We need your phone!"

They pounded and pounded, but eventually they had to accept that it was no use. Nobody was going to come to the door. Cyrus and Buffy looked at each other, beyond miserable, and then wandered back across the porch to where Andi was standing.

"That's it, then," Cyrus practically sobbed, the slightest hint of anger flashing in his dark eyes. "We're never leaving here."

But Buffy was beyond furious. "Why did you do that?" she demanded, glaring at Andi.

Andi did feel terrible, but she wouldn't let the guilt stop her from trying to make things right. "You heard what Bex said. . . ." Andi pasted a determined smile on her face. "When we want to make something happen, we make it happen!"

"Live update," Buffy said, her voice dripping with disdain. "We did *not* re-create our best day ever!"

"We still can!" Andi insisted. "I don't know how, I know the odds are against us . . . *severely* against us, but . . . you're moving," Andi continued, her eyes pleading with Buffy to get back on board. "And I don't want you to remember us giving up. I want you to remember us as the kids who made it happen!"

Buffy's face began to soften. How could she possibly stay mad at Andi when she was so committed to re-creating their perfect day—a day that would, quite possibly, be one of the last the three friends would ever spend together? In some ways, Buffy couldn't help feeling like some of her own tenacious grit had rubbed off on Andi—and then she felt a pang of pride as she thought about the fact that Andi might even be a worthy contender to carry on Buffy's overachieving legacy after she left town.

But while Buffy was finally coming around, Cyrus

was moving in the opposite direction, driven largely by the fact that the mud covering the vast majority of his body was beginning to harden . . . and itch.

"That's a very stirring speech," Cyrus told Andi, "but I have to wonder if you'd make it if you had only one shoe. Because I don't see how this day could possibly get any—"

Before Cyrus could finish his thought, a buzzing noise interrupted him and then a bee dove through the air and flew directly into his left cheek—stinging fast and stinging hard.

"Ahhh! Ow!" Cyrus screamed, slapping his own face as Andi and Buffy looked on in horror. "Ow, ow, ow! Curse my sweet blood!"

Andi cringed and looked at her friends, hoping against hope that she might still be able to convince them to revive their plan. Because she refused to believe that, after all they'd already been through, a tiny flying insect would wind up being the thing that stopped them from re-creating their perfect day.

CHAPTER 8

It hadn't been easy, but in between Cyrus's sobs, Andi had somehow talked her friends into making one last-ditch attempt to walk to the Alpine Slide. As she trekked a few paces ahead of them up a hill that she *hoped* was a shortcut, she heard Cyrus complaining. Again.

"Yes?" Buffy asked through gritted teeth while trudging through the tall yellow grass, carrying Cyrus on her back.

"Your shoulder is digging into my side," Cyrus whined.

"Oh, I'm *sorry*," Buffy fired back. "Maybe it's because *your whole body is digging into* my *body*."

"Point taken," Cyrus replied with a sigh, wrapping his arms more tightly around Buffy's shoulders. "Carry on."

When Andi finally got to the top of the hill, she breathed a sigh of relief. There, off in the distance, was the paved road that would take them to the Alpine Slide. Then a familiar blue pickup truck that had been cruising along the road pulled over. It had a bunch of plants and trees loaded into the back. It was the Judy's Blooms truck!

"Bex?" Andi practically squealed, in spite of herself.

"It's Buffy, actually," Buffy muttered, not yet seeing what Andi saw as she got to the top of the hill with Cyrus still weighing her down.

"No, *Bex*!" Andi pointed to the truck and started to run. Buffy quickly dropped Cyrus, and all three of them raced down the hill.

"Does someone need a Mack-sy Taxi?" Bex asked with a wink after opening the door and stepping out. As relieved and happy as Andi was to see her, she couldn't help rolling her eyes at Bex's lame joke. "Sorry, it just popped into my head on the drive over, and I had to say it to someone."

Andi smiled and shook her head, putting her hands on her hips and marveling at Bex. She looked like an extremely cool real-life superhero, strutting toward Andi and her friends in her black leather jacket and heavy motorcycle boots.

"How did you know to come get us?" Andi asked.

"Something sounded off about your phone call," Bex explained as she slowly scanned each mud-covered kid from head to toe. "And I thought I heard Cyrus . . . crying . . . in the background?"

"Cyrus saves the day!" Cyrus noted with a shrug, glancing over at Buffy. "Not something you get to say very often."

As Buffy laughed at Cyrus, Bex looked down at his feet and asked, "Why do you only have one shoe?" Then, glancing from Cyrus to Andi to Buffy, she added, "And *zero* bikes?"

"Well . . ." Andi sucked in her breath and held it there.

"Never mind, you can explain later," Bex interjected. She'd been through her fair share of adventures-gone-wrong and knew exactly how Andi and her friends had to be feeling at that particular moment. There weren't a lot of words she could say to make them feel better, so she went with the first ones that came to her: "I'm just glad you're safe."

Andi smiled gratefully. "Thanks, Mom."

Bex grinned. But she could also hear the defeat in Andi's voice, and she was eager to do whatever she could to help. "So . . ." she said, studying the three grimy faces in front of her. "Where do you want to go?"

Looking at each other, Andi and her friends didn't even need to discuss it, let alone say it out loud—they could completely read each other's minds, and their next stop was an obvious choice.

CHAPTER 9

Finally perched on their favorite stools at The Spoon, still windblown and covered in dried mud, Andi and Buffy breathed a sigh of relief while Cyrus held an ice pack to his bee sting. As they savored every greasy bite of their baby taters, a waitress walked past and scowled at them, veering as far away from their spot at the counter as she could possibly get.

"We don't look *that* bad," Andi called after the waitress, offended that anyone would make such an obvious effort to avoid her and her friends.

"Oh, I think we do," Buffy noted, laughing as she gestured at their filthy coats and faces—and especially at the ice pack Cyrus had on his face.

Andi laughed, too, but then she grew serious. "Look," she said, blinking remorsefully at Buffy, "I know it wasn't the best day ever . . . but promise me you won't think of it as the *worst*?"

"I won't," Buffy agreed with a grin, grabbing Andi by the shoulder and laughing again. "Maybe just the *craziest*."

Cyrus laughed, too, and Andi said, "I can live with that," as she popped another baby tater into her mouth.

She was bummed that they hadn't made it to the Alpine Slide—that they hadn't *exactly* re-created their perfect day—but, as Cyrus had pointed out, the moment their bikes were stolen, they had entered new territory.

Just then, the little bell on the door of The Spoon jingled and Andi and her friends turned around to see a couple of familiar-looking kids coming in, one of them in a tan beanie and the other pulling off a black bicycle helmet and setting it on the front table. It was the two teenagers they'd seen earlier, when they were in Deputy Bartlett's car—but now they were both wearing white Alpine Slide souvenir T-shirts with blue letters that said, *WHOOSH* YOU WERE HERE!

"It *can't* be," Andi gasped.

"Those are the guys who stole our bikes!" Cyrus whispered.

"*And* our day!" Buffy added under her breath as the two teenagers walked obliviously past them. "Did you see what they were wearing? The Alpine Slide T-shirts!"

As the full gravity of the situation hit him, Cyrus slammed his fists on the countertop. "Are we going to just sit here and let them take our day? *No! We are not those kids!* We are going to reclaim what's ours! Who's with me?"

"I am!" Buffy yelled, placing her hand on Cyrus's.

"Me too!" Andi agreed, laying a hand on top of Buffy's

"*Let's go!*" Cyrus said, his voice low but commanding as they all jumped up from the counter and grabbed the bike helmet from the front table before storming outside.

When they got to the bike racks in front of The Spoon, Andi and Cyrus each hopped on one of the bikes while Buffy peeked through the window of the diner to make sure the teenagers hadn't followed them. She motioned for Andi and Cyrus to hurry—the coast was clear!

Andi and Cyrus quickly rode off while Buffy ran alongside them. As they raced down Main Street, exhilarated, Buffy shouted, "Ha! We win!"

"We got our day back!" Andi yelled.

Grinning from ear to ear, they continued their victory ride until Cyrus suddenly paused and looked down at his bike, concerned. "Um . . . guys?"

They all slowed to a stop.

Andi frowned and looked down, too. "These . . . aren't our bikes, are they?" she asked.

Buffy grimaced and shook her head. "Nope."

As a panicked look flashed across Cyrus's face, the three friends stared at each other, wondering what to do next. After a long, terrified pause, they all suddenly burst out laughing—louder and harder than they had in their entire lives. Even more than they had after buying the little license plates at the cider stand!

As Buffy threw back her head and Cyrus doubled over, tears of happiness streamed down Andi's flushed cheeks once again.

"It doesn't matter what we do . . ." Cyrus finally said when the laughter died down.

"As long as we're together," Andi said, completing the thought.

They all nodded, smiling giddily at each other. But then Buffy's face clouded over. "Which . . . will only be for another week," she added sadly.

Cyrus felt like he'd just been punched in the stomach. "Wow," he gasped as he looked into Buffy's eyes. "I actually forgot."

"Me too." Andi could barely squeak out the words as she looked at her friends, all three of them now fighting back tears.

After standing there in silence for what felt like hours, Buffy finally pasted on a smile and straightened up. Andi had definitely inherited plenty of her tenacity, and now it was up to Buffy to make sure she continued to set the best possible example . . . right up until her very last day in Shadyside.

"See you tomorrow?" Buffy said, digging deeper than ever to find her resilience.

Andi and Cyrus slowly nodded.

"Tomorrow," Andi whispered.

Then, before they headed their separate ways, Buffy leaned in and wrapped one arm around each of her friends, and they fell into a group hug—the longest hug the three of them had ever shared. They knew that they were going to have to let go, but none of them wanted to. Not now. Not ever.

Eventually, though, they did break apart, and Buffy flashed an awkward smile as Andi and Cyrus turned to wheel their stolen bikes back over to the rack in front of The Spoon.

Then Buffy headed back to her house.

Alone.